WRITERS REPUBLIC

THE
IN BETWEEN

KAYLEE DIAL

WRITERS REPUBLIC L.L.C.
515 Summit Ave. Unit R1
Union City, NJ 07087, USA

Website: *www.writersrepublic.com*
Hotline: *1-877-656-6838*
Email: *info@writersrepublic.com*

Ordering Information:
Quantity sales. Special discounts are available on quantity purchases by corporations, associations, and others. For details, contact the publisher at the address above.

Library of Congress Control Number: 2021915639
ISBN-13:   978-1-63728-451-3   [Paperback Edition]
                  978-1-63728-452-0   [Digital Edition]

Rev. date: 08/20/2021

I dedicate this novel to my senior year Creative Writing teacher, Mr. Campbell. He barely knew me when I started in his class and yet from the moment he read my first short story in his class he did everything he could to inspire me to continue in the field of writing. He told me I had something special and that he wouldn't be surprised to find my books in stores one day, and I hope he was right and if seeing this, is proud.

Without him, I'm not sure I would have taken the final step to deciding my future career as an author, or even had the courage to do it. It also helps that I wrote this novel in his class rather than doing my other school work most of the time. So thank you Mr. Campbell, I hope I've made you proud.

CHAPTER

1

They say it's peaceful when you die. Quiet and quick. That your life flashes before your eyes and you relive all that made you who you are... were. Well I, Maeve Cowen, can tell you... that is not the case. I remember my death like it was yesterday, though it was exactly twenty years ago. The day I lost everything...

It was 1997 and I was walking home from a late shift down at the print shop. I remember the sharp bite to the air and how it chilled me to the bone. My heavy coat did nothing to stop the ferocious wind from beating my body. My feet pounded against the cobblestone path, matching the quickened thump of my heart. I remember the snow as it fell from the sky, almost like hardened tears gliding through the air, melting down my face. It was dark, too dark for my liking. The street lamps were dim and far apart and it seemed there were moments where I wouldn't find another, even one to cast a slight shadow. I suppose my shivering caused my teeth to clatter so loudly I was prevented from hearing my approaching death as it rattled down the street, angrily screeching, an unacknowledged warning sliding over the iced pavement.

It was too late by the time I noticed the unnatural flare of light behind me and in seconds I was hit. This grand metal beast devoured my innocent flesh ruthlessly until I lay scarlett against the pale of the snow. I could feel every painful breath being stripped from my body. Suddenly, I stood over my broken, mutilated body. Desperately I wrapped my arms around myself, hoping to offer some semblance of comfort. Falling back to the ground, a scream ripped free from my ghostly throat, tearing through the air until the wind rampaged alongside my misery.

Moments passed before I heard the deafening crunch of snow under boots, running closer and closer. I peeled my eyes away from my death to the one who approached. He was young and clearly terrified. His blonde hair nearly matched the color of the snow. His tall personage fell down next to me, the dying me. I wanted to scream at him, "*Get help!*" but before I could say anything, he spoke.

"Shit!" he yelped, clearly understanding the atrocity occurring right before his eyes. I watched him fumble as he wondered whether he should attempt to stop the bleeding, scream for help, or just *run away*. As time unforgivingly slipped away, I felt the connection between my body, and whatever I had become, severing. It was the worst pain I had ever felt. It was like I was being hit by the car over and over again, helpless as my skin burned and peeled away from my bones. My brain was on fire, my eyes feeling like pincushions pierced without mercy. It was a boring pain... one so fierce it scorched itself into my memory even after all sensation had left me for good. It became a phantom pain and an intimate reminder of how it felt to die. How it felt to watch my humanity be ripped from my fingers. Instantly all I was, was a helpless soul, left to traverse the Earth in search of relief from this new existence - if you could even call it that - something I believed would only come from finding the one who killed me. It only took me twenty years.

It's the twentieth anniversary of my death and the days seem to offer homage, the sun covering itself in a thick, black cloak of drunken clouds. There's a familiar chill to the air but I can't feel the Ann Arbor rain, like glass, against my pale skin. My eyes are unable to water at the whip of the wind. I've travelled to many places since dying, my focus has remained narrow in my search. None of those towns or cities provided relief for me, of this fact I wasn't surprised. It would make sense for my ghostly self to continuously be pulled back to the city where I lost everything. And it helped that the ambiance of this town matched my lack

3

of humanity in a sense. Because of this, I decided I would come back here once my mission is complete and I'm not shuttled off to heaven, or hell for that matter. Who knows what rules are put against a phantom murderess.

I chuckle to myself, accustomed to the echo of my voice against the invisible boundary that separates me from the living. Classic to a novelists description, they can't see, hear, or touch me. I mean, I can't exactly touch them or the rest of the tangible world either, but I am able to fully manipulate the suggestive states of their minds, which is how I plan to enact my vengeance.

I spend the rest of this dreary day drowning in memories of my death. They always seems to magnify ten fold on the anniversary and this only helps ignite the fire of hatred that gives me a purpose. I glide, inhumanly, through the air, pushing myself through people and relishing in the brief flirtation of breath that flows from them and courses through my viel of a being. I found this ability a year into my time being "dead". It felt like a spark of adrenaline. Not quite unlike the one you get when you're shot down the highest peak of a roller coaster, when the air fills your lungs and there is a plummet in your stomach that fills with the buzz of excited energy. The thrill of living. I don't know how it works and, really, I don't care, I just know that I feel alive when I touch them, even if they are mocking me with their pure humanity. Why couldn't I keep that feeling for myself, or just a little longer? Something to make me feel not so… empty.

As I'm thinking this, I find myself in the middle of an empty street. I generally avoid cars, considering one assisted the driver who caused my death. Suddenly, feeling brave knowing there are no metal animals en route, I find myself pulled into a haunting dance, the wind acting as my music. I bend and bow, twirl and glide as the wind matches me in time and torture. The howling sounds fill my ears and I lose myself to it. My washed out long black hair tangling as it strikes at the empty air around me, wrapping and unwrapping as I spin and tumble across the cobbled street.

In a rude interruption of my mournful dance, something slices through the air, pulling me out of my captivated state. "Watch out!" he screams with caution. His deep voice strangled by trepidation. I turn to face him, curious as to the source of his outburst. Suddenly, I find myself face to face with the most gorgeous person I have ever seen. His enchanting blue eyes gazing fiercely into mine, now a faded grey. His white blonde hair falling about his face, framing it with a natural wave. Startled, I avoid contact as he comes shuttling towards me, muscled arms opened to embrace me in a sort of tackle. He looks surprised when I step aside and watches me as he overshoots and falls onto the unforgiving street. As he collides with the pavement, dumbfounded, I realize that he was trying to save me.

I feel it move through me. An old familiar sensation tangible colliding with the intangible. The car moves through me in a second, but I'm so shocked I collapse to my knees, still in the middle of the street. I put my hands up to my head and just stay there, my eyes widened. I'm not physically hurt, that just wouldn't be possible, but memories flood the space around me suffocating and trapping me in an unappreciated remembrance.

"What the f-?" he exclaims, staring me down as I shoot my head up to look at him. He looks utterly confused but there's no fear in his eyes. His confusion morphs into disbelief as he looks from me, crouching on the ground, to the where the car had gone. "That car hit you! Why aren't you…" he trails off as he takes a moment to really see me.

Not expecting him to hear me, I jest to myself. "Come on Casinova, I'm sure you're not just pretty."

"Well, you're right, but I don't usually watch someone get hit by a car and then not be affected by it," he snaps back. It's obvious my backhanded compliment struck a nerve.

I stare at him, wide-eyed. "You can hear me?" I question, slowly bringing myself into a standing position. My loosely fitted, dingy white dress matches my movements as I straighted and take a couple steps towards him.

He makes no attempt to stop me and continues to stare like before as I saunter towards him. He watches me like I'm a jewel. Something he wants to grab ahold of and never let go. I feel a slight pang of jealousy as I recognize a growing relief in his eyes. This relief seemed like it meant he had finally found the thing he's been looking for forever, and that thing was me. I wondered what he saw to look at me this way. It is apparent that he can see my body, with a translucent shimmer, my silhouette blurred by the wistful wind. He can see my unnaturally long black hair and muted pale-rose complexion. My graceful dancers feet move me towards him, making false steps across the pavement. He shudders and I'm am left to decipher whether it's the frozen air or me that elicits the reaction.

Trying to take my time in approaching him, I quickly realize that I can't stay away any longer. I am drawn to him. Is this because of his god-like looks or his attempt at heroics to save a dead girl? Or is it because after all this time, someone finally saw me? The connection was ultimately unexplainable but this didn't stop me from kneeling down to stare directly into his eyes once reaching him. I hoped they would give me some answers and I take it to mean he's just as absorbed by me as I am by him when he doesn't draw away from me.

"You can't be real, can you?" he asks breathlessly. His eyes hungrily scan over me. "A fairy? An angel?"

I can't help the laugh that bubbles from my chest at the romantic way he describes me. The laugh produces an echo that surrounds us in our own momentary universe. I watch his ears flush with the red hugh that accompanies human embarrassment. We've only just met, but somehow we seem to effect each other in an astronomical way.

"I'm nothing pure like those things," I say, curious when my voice heightens in pitch. I remembered this as something I used to do while I was alive and would flirt.

It's not surprising that I would find this boy attractive, he's gorgeous, and definitely my type, but I never thought I could feel anything like this in my current state. I never really felt this way about anyone when I was a living, breathing, person. I could feel the tension in the air around his form, constricting and flexing as I imagined his muscles would. He was moving now and in moments he was towering above me. His hair falls into his mesmerizing, sky tainted, eyes and I can't look away. There's a strike like lightning burning through my chest the longer his gaze holds me in its focus. It doesn't feel bad, but I am disturbed by the sensations. They are too much for me to handle, considering they are the first I've felt in twenty years!

Suddenly I'm overwhelmed with the desperate urge for familiarity, anything to remove myself from this moment... from him. Coldly I find myself dismissing him. "Well, I should probably get back to doing my ghostly things." He doesn't say anything, so I take that as an acknowledgement and start to leave.

"Wait!" he calls and I turn back to him just as he's reaching out to me. His hand glides roughly through the empty space where the figment of my arm lies. The immediate rush of his electricity wracks my being. The aura of his living energy courses like blood through a vein, searing like sparklers up my arms. My false skin under his hand fades from its pale complexion and glows unnaturally bright gold. It takes all I have to look away from our hands to his stunned face. I'm shaken to my core as I feel the full force of the moment weighing down on me. Every second I remain here, touching him like this, I can feel how my energy slowly starts to dissipate. "Hey... hey!" he cries out, catching my limp body as I cascade towards the cobblestones.

As if in retaliation for breeching the supernatural laws, I am enveloped in utter darkness. There are unspoken rules, the living cannot touch the dead. It couldn't have been more than a few moments before my eyes slowly work open again, I find myself lying in the middle of nothingness. Disoriented I scan the black void, searching for something that offers stability in the moment. But it's to no avail. I regress, selling myself the suffocation of solitude once more, a fate I accept.

I am about to give up and accept my fate when suddenly, I'm blinded by a bang of light, one that devours the darkness. I can feel my phantom soaking in the energy of the light, as it draws me in. A seductive, whispering voice comes from the center of the light, like a chorus calling out to me. Unfamiliar echos of men, women, and children. I feel hands, each a figment of an almost reality, grasp my arms and pull me in. Closer and closer to the brightness. I don't try and stop them, it feels easier to do nothing. For the second time, even for an instant, I feel something other than vengeance and death. Dare I say, for a moment, I feel alive.

Just as I reach the light, barely a step from the promises that await me on the other side, I hear my name rebound off the walls of the void and come smashing down on me. I'm thrown out of my trance and stumble unforgivingly away from the bewitching brightness. Those hopeful hands draw back into the light in retaliation to my rejection. I am cast back into the disorienting darkness and immediately begin searching hopelessly for the other voice, for the entity that called my name.

In the next unexplainable moment, I am slowly returning to consciousness, laying on the floor of the void and overwhelmed with a daunting familiarity. Again I loose myself, my conscious self and just as quickly as I find myself disappearing, I am laying in the arms of that living boy. The one that tried to save me from that car.

"Maeve, Maeve are you okay?" he calls to me but I'm too distracted by my skin, glowing gold on top of his to acknowledge his questioning. Every spot where his hand is in contact with my phantom glimmers radiantly.

"I'm fine, relax," I snap at him, still disoriented and longing for the light, yet feeling an odd sense of warmth wherever he touches me. All I can do is just sit there, in his arms. Wracked with surprise within the next moment, I realize something as I look into his worried blue eyes. "How do you know my name?" I jerk out of his arms and force myself to stand.

"You, you said it while you were… unconscious? Asleep? You said your name was Maeve Cowen and you… vowed to get revenge on your murder…" he says, slowly down halfway through his statement to soak in what those words actually meant. "You were murdered?"

"Yes, I was murdered," I spit with venom on the tip of my tongue. It's not my intention to be mean to him exactly, it's a necessary evil. I can't allow this *living boy* to distract me any longer and I don't want to waste my time when I have something more important to do. Maybe when I'm done with all of that, I can come back and decipher why he is able to dampen my vengeful spirit. Or perhaps why he clouds my emotions with whatever it is, peace or who knows. But who can say for sure, maybe I'll never see him again. "Well, it was interesting to meet you... uhh. Maybe I'll see you around some day."

His energy literally falls to match his saddened features at my blatant rejection. *But of what part?* I can't help but wonder. His concern or maybe his extension of kindness. "I see..." is all he says. He slumps his head up and down as his almost heavy stature starts away from me, leaving me standing alone and unseen in the groggy street. *It's better this way.* I turn my back to him now, not willing to watch as the only person that has seen me since my death disappears behind the dense fog, molding into another shadow on the empty road. I know I won't be able to forget him, his ability to make me glow on both the inside and outside is something I could never let go. But I must erase him from my memory in order to focus on my karmic task. I recognize it will be in vain as his memory burns into my consciousness. I will move on then, as I resume my vengeful wandering, but he won't be far from the peak of my thoughts. I was with him for such a brief time, but he left an impression, and decided I'd have to see him again.

CHAPTER

2

It's been a long, tedious month. A month with no success in finding my killer and a month since I was seen. I find myself begrudgingly taking steps forward, once again pondering my time stuck in a haze of revenge, confusion and the unquenchable desire to find *him* again. For a brief moment, I hear the wind, which was previously blowing in a gentle song, waiver as a familiar voice reaches my ears. I feel my metaphorical heart squeeze in my chest. *It's him*, I think to myself as my gaze shoots like a bullet towards his charming laughter.

He stands tall and relaxed. The air around him beckons me closer. I obey, nearly floating towards him, needing to be nearer. Suddenly, he turns in my direction and I duck behind a pillar. This market is drenched with random pillars. It was the first thing I thought of, to shield myself from his unwanted attention. Though now I feel like an idiot, a ghostly being hiding from a living human. Can he even see me anymore anyways? The thought pierces me but I push it away in order to focus on him. But what catches my gaze now, is the girl standing with him, following him like a lost puppy. She causes a jealous fire to burn the air surrounding me.

I can't stand it when he says something to her and I hear her flitty laughter dance between them. Newly motivated by emotions I don't understand, I slowly trespass into their space just as she puts a flirtatious hand on his forearm. I sneer and move up behind him, peaking my head around his shoulder so he can clearly see me. It takes him a moment, but when his eyes lock on mine and I watch them widen followed by a sharp intake of breath, I revel in satisfaction. He doesn't speak to me, instead he composes himself and turns away from me to continue his conversation with the girl, acting as though he never saw me. Their conversation drags on in a tense discussion of unimportant *"living"* things. I decide to once again insert myself in order to be noticed by him. Walking in front of them with a teasing laugh echoing in my throat, I know I've won when he flexes and flinches towards me when I fall back into him, like a trust fall. The game is fun for me until he sends the obnoxious girl on her way. I am distracted and in the middle of a backwards lean when he suddenly wraps his arms around mine. A phantom shiver escapes my intangible body as my translucent skin glows golden as it had before. I can't exactly feel his skin on mine, but I can sense his vibrating energy. I am curious and don't pull away.

He takes a set of deep breaths that seem to reverberate throughout me. Slowly, the vibrating energy grows, which to me translate that he is squeezing me tighter. He leads us out of the middle of the market and into a quieter, less trafficked space.

"I thought it would be better for us to talk in private," he says at last, pulling away from me and putting a respectful amount of distance between us. I narrow my brows at this separation, but decide it would be best to ignore it since we don't really know each other yet.

"Who was that girl you were with?" I interrogate him. Both of us taken aback by the jealousy in my voice. Probably not the best way to start off a conversation but what can I do about it now?

His beautiful face contorts nervously as his eyes dance, landing everywhere but on me. "She's a girl I know from school."

"Okay," I reply, shrugging my shoulders as a means to regain composure. This is obviously not the response he expected and he gives me a weird look.

"I seriously don't understand you," he states, exasperated.

"I don't understand myself either," I shrug.

He groans. "What do you want with me? First you basically tell me to leave you alone, I don't see or hear anything from you in a month, and then our second meeting goes like this! It's confusing. I spent weeks trying to convince myself you didn't exist just to stop myself from look for you!"

I sigh and look away from him. I can't say I'm embarrassed by my actions, death is too weird to be embarrassed about stupid things like that. "I just spotted you and I couldn't help myself from approaching you," I answer truthfully. "There is something about you that peaks my interest. It's not just that you are unnaturally attractive with that snow hair and those gravitational blue eyes or even that you make my skin glow when you touch me... there's... I-I don't know," I conclude.

"How could I possibly interest you? We've met one time and I'm pretty positive you don't even know my name," he says. "But... that's not to say I'm not intrigued by you either," he continues, his voice unsure.

"You have a point there," I refer to the fact that I actually don't know his name. "Well, since you know mine, what is yours?"

"Kian Siclair," he responds almost immediately.

"Kian Sinclair..." I ponder the name. "That sounds like the popular, football star you'd find in high school," I giggle to myself, picturing it. The football jersey, the swarm of girls... and guys for that matter, drooling over this god of a boy.

He smiles awkwardly and rubs the back of his neck with his hand. "You got me there," he chuckles and my mouth drops open. Of course he is. "I'm the captain of the football team and I get along with a lot of people at my school-"

"A humble way of saying you are admired by everyone around you," I interrupt and he rolls his eyes playfully.

"Well, if you know so much about me, what's your story?" he shoots back and I find myself drawn silent, staring at him.

He seems to notice my weird response and calls attention to it. "You don't have to tell me if it makes you uncomfortable..." I offer a weak smile and I know he sees right through it.

"It's fine. I suppose I could tell you," I murmur thinking back to how I merely blurted out I was murdered and then sent him away last time.

"It was twenty years ago and I was walking home from a late shift at my part-time job when..." and slowly, I ease my way into the story of my death, offering every gruesome detail even as I explain my final mission. When I come to a natural conclusion, I take a moment for myself before I look at the boy I'm sure I've just scarred for life, if he hasn't already been considering, he's talking to a ghost right now.

"I want to help," Kian states and my head shoots up to stare at him, shocked.

"You what?" I demand, narrowing my eyes at him suspiciously.

"I want to help you," he confirms his previous statement.

"You... you can't..." I start but am interrupted by his hand as he holds the face of his palm up to stop me.

"I don't mean help you murder whoever hurt you. I meant, I want to help you find your humanity... or help you feel human again and hopefully you won't need to hurt anyone else," he clarifies and I'm silent. I watch him with predatory, grey eyes. He doesn't push the matter, but I can see the astute resolution on his face and, with a nearing thirty-eight years of experience, I know there is no use fighting him.

"I see your mind's made up and I know what I'm going to say will be pointless, but I don't want to drag you into my personal affairs. I'm giving you an out now, before I agree to anything," I warn. He doesn't give anything away and I feel slightly revived at his sure desire to help me. I realize I was never going to say no to him, I've been alone too long to deny his companionship and I can tell he made the same assumption.

"No need," he confirms. "I am going to help you until you don't need me anymore. I will give you the most human life a dead person can have!" His handsome face grows meticulously into a righteous smile and I can't help but respond with my own take on a feigned vomit. I can see him rolling his eyes out of the corner of my own and I do my best not to look. I'm absolutely useless when he does that.

"So, what should we do today then?" he asks, not allowing time for an awkward pause.

"I don't know. I was eighteen in 1997, sure I tried to keep up with the change in human life up to this point, but I can't say I cared too much. I have my mind set on another task," I remind him, folding my arms across my chest. I can't help but notice the expression that crosses his face when I tell him the year I died, but I am quick to brush away the memory.

"Right..." he says. It doesn't take him long to bring back up his spirits and he straightens his shoulders. "Well, as a popular, eighteen-year-old in 2018, I'm sure I can show you a good time."

I smirk at him. *I'm sure if I was alive you could*, I think to myself, unashamed by my blatant desire for him. A few moments pass in silence, me contemplating scenarios that are too inappropriate, yet satisfying, to speak aloud, and him thinking who knows what.

Suddenly, his eyes grow to the size of bowling balls and his once innocent face darkens to a shade of red I didn't know was possible. "I-I didn't mean 'show you a good...' I mean... I want to help you with your humanity situation, of course, not... no wait I don't mean I'm thinking about that... I am you are very beautiful... but-"

I cut him off with my laughter. Surprised that he would be so abashed about an accidental innuendo. "Are you always like this?" I ask him, wiping pretend tears from my eyes as my bubbly laughter loosens.

He looks offended as he responds. "Of course not. It's… just different with you." Mimicking my previous stance, he crosses his fold his arms over his chest, driving his point home. My laughter grows more in my throat at this. He reminds me of a child pouting over a lost argument. However, to not add insult to injury, I swallow it back down. I know he catches on to my struggle though. "Whatever, I'm hungry," he murmurs as he turns away from me and back to the busy street.

I follow close behind him, watching the way he walks, gaining in confidence as he strides down the street. Despite being so embarrassed just a moment ago, he commands the space he walks through easily and I somehow find it quite appealing. Feeling dazed, I realize I have to know more about this boy. More about what he likes and dislikes, what he does on the daily to keep himself occupied, what his life is like. The girl from earlier pops into my head for a brief moment and that just makes me want to know more about who she was to him, or if there is someone special in his life already. There's so much I have to know. I smile at myself, feeling silly for already feeling so possessive and close to him.

"A penny for your thoughts," Kian says, bringing my attention back towards him in an instant.

I'm not ashamed of my feelings or my thoughts for that matter, but I don't feel like sharing them… not yet. "What did you want to eat? You said you were hungry," I say, obviously avoiding his earlier inquiry.

He raises a curious brow at me. Shrugging his shoulders, he follows along, probably realizing I wasn't going to say anything else. "I don't know. How about burgers?" he asks, looking for my preference.

"Considering I can't eat, it's really up to you, dear." Goofily, he whacks his forehead with his palm and I can't help but giggle at the boyish action.

"Duh. That makes sense." He laughs along with me and we set off in small talk until we reach the first inviting diner.

Kian requests a booth near the back of the restaurant to limit unwanted attention. The hostess tries quickly to change Kian's mind on the seating arrangement, trying to find a better fit for "a single diner", but to no avail. Within minutes we are seated in our back booth and Kian has placed his order. Once his food is put on the table, I can't help but gawk at it. The most steamingly tremendous, gargantuan burger I have ever seen rests tastefully in front of him. If only I had the capability I know my mouth would be watering at the sight of the medium rare patty, greasy and fulfilling, the crispy cold blanket of lettuce, the melted cheddar cheese practically dripping off the sides of the toasted bun.

I shake my head in order to distract myself from the familiarity of the comfort food and for a while we sit in silence. As he eats, a questions plays in my brain. I ponder it for a moment but when it starts toiling I decide to force it out. "Why do you want to help me?" The words coil between us, like a serpent ready to strike if it's not handled the right way.

After the seconds tick by without a response, I feel an emotional numbness come over me, greeting me like an old friend. More time allows this numbness to fester into anger and I start to feel like the serpent, the one that Kian's just poked with a sharp stick. Before I can react to his neutral stare he replies. "Frankly, I don't know. I'm honestly shocked by all of this. I'm in turmoil, dabbling in something unnatural. The living able to see the dead? You sit there nonchalantly, like this is something you do all of the time." I feel out of breath for him considering the speed at which his words fly from his mouth.

I stare at him slack-jawed. I haven't seen him this blatantly bewildered before, he's usually so confident. I actually half expected him to pull a cliche move and say something cheesy about being a hero destined to help a damsel in distress. I ponder for a moment, understanding that this may be too hard for him. He clearly is the most unselfish guy I have ever met and considering he has no ulterior motive behind helping me, some random dead girl, it makes me question if I should let this continue any further. I will get my revenge one way or another, despite any futile attempt to 'guide me in the humane direction'. For now, I simply let him eat his burger in peace. Once he capably inhales his food, he wipes his hands and settles into a pose of utmost sincerity. In reaction, I feel as though

I need to dab away a cold sweat from my forehead, if that was physically possible of course.

"What is it?" I ask, as blatant and straightforward as he seems to be.

"I know how I can help you regain your humanity," he replies, folding his strong hands in front of him and staring deeply into my eyes. It feels like he is seeing right through me and that makes me momentarily uneasy.

"Do you now?" I scoff back, the sarcasm triggered in my voice an unstoppable reaction to his unbreaking solemnity.

"In fact I do," he scoffs back teasingly. I can't help but laugh at the sudden game of sarcastic wit that breaks the tension of our conversation. Imagine, a ghost regaining her humanity with the help of a human boy who has no sane reason to get involved or any idea what it means to get involved with the supernatural.

"Well, spit it out then," I say, my hands moving in a gesture that says 'lay it all on the table'.

He clears his throat proudly then settles in to his plan. "I'm going to take you to all the most human attractions I can find," he states, "starting with the fair that is going on these next few months."

I raise my eyebrows and resist the urge to roll my eyes. "I don't see how that will reintroduce me to being a human," I comment, disinterested.

"Don't knock the idea before you give it a chance." I can tell he's being coy as he extends an alluring hand. "Besides, I'm confident this will work."

"Based off of what?" I float my own hand above his, not touching but close enough that both of us recognize a familiar vibrating feeling. It's muted as we aren't making full contact but it's still there and it causes Kian's face to color in embarrassment.

"Oh... it's nothing really. It works in the movies so..."

Feeling I've gotten the upper hand, I stare at him blankly for a moment and his discomfort grows. He squirms in his seat under my unyielding glare. I can hold out only a moment longer before my body explodes with thunderous heaps of laughter. His eyes widen in shock and his jaw drops open at my assault to his plan, and more importantly, his pride.

"If you don't like my plan we can think of something else," he shrugs. His voice deep with irritation and he withdraws his hand.

I'm caught off guard by the way his voice nearly growls at me and I can all but feel the vibrations of his emotion coursing through my ghostly veins. My laughter comes to a disintegrating halt and I reassure him by shaking my head. Feeling suddenly ashamed for my manipulation of him, I hurry to take it back.

"No, I'm sorry. It's not like I've thought of anything better these last twenty years-" *and it's not like anything he tries is going to change my mind.* Revenge is the only way to satisfy the twenty years of burning hatred that consumes me and is the only thing that gives me form outside of my lost humanity.

As I feel both our thoughts racing over the tornado of emotions, I decide it's time for me to take my leave. I have to wander to get my mind straightened out before concluding whether or not I should be around this boy. There is a lot we are testing here outside of the strict boundary of the living and dead, of afterlife. Even just by speaking with each other we are probably breaking so many cosmic rules. Honestly, it's not even me I'm concerned about, I'm already dead. I can't impose my fate on him considering not even I know what he stands to lose here. I stand and move away from him, phasing through the wall of the restaurant into the outdoors, putting a wall of distance between us. I am trying not to look back at the booth where he stays for only a moment before calling to me through the glass.

"Wait! Maeve?" he calls and I hear his pounding footsteps against the cobblestone, music to my ears. I turn to find him directly in front of me again, the distance I had previously put between us has been closed in seconds. "How will I know how to reach you?" he questions, his jaw set as if he's preparing for a blow to the face.

I smile mischievously at him. "You won't. I will find you."

CHAPTER

3

And that I did, though it took me another two months before I decided to look for Kian again. He had been on my mind persistently and it was slowly driving me crazy. He was distracting me, so I decided, amidst my search for the one who left me for dead, I would know where Kian was and what he was doing. What surprised me the most, was how I needed to know how he was. He shouldn't have that much control over me. I suppose it makes some sense, he's the only other being that knows of my existence. So I can make time for him, it's not like there is a timed limitation for my endgame either way.

Today as he walks to school, I trail behind him for a minute. Mentally debating how I will make my grand re-appearance. Just as I am about to call out to him, no planned greeting perfect enough to offer this special moment justice, someone else gets to him first.

"Kian!" she calls from across the street. I turn my head to see who it is and I recognize the girl from the marketplace.

"Hey Giselle," he replies casually, offering a twitch of his wrist as a wave.

"Mind if I walk with you today?" she questions, already skipping towards him like a love-struck puppy. I take a moment to scan her, with her tanned, freckled body, flirtatious short blonde hair and slim dancer's figure.

"'Course," he answers, his lips pulling into a tight, friendly smile.

I fall back like a shadow, watching them. I hate that she looks good next to him. The farther ahead they get, I feel a new pressure in my phantasmic body, a strange sensation considering I can't generally feel *anything* physically. They take additional steps away, increasing the distance between us, and the pressure grows causing my brain to throb uncontrollably. *What the hell?* I think, trying to hurriedly determine what this means.

"So, Mae- Giselle!" I hear Kian correct himself, realizing he was about to call out my name. My eyes zone in on him and I am drawn closer to him. With each step forward the pressure begins to dim significantly.

Is he calling to me? I ponder silently, taking yet another step. The pressure is gone now that I am practically invading his personal space, nearly touching his strong back. My thoughts stray as I think back over the last two months and pinpoint multiple occasions when I felt a pain similar to this. Every time I simply dismissed it, not making the connection to him until now. I suppose it's possible he could possess this ability to tie me to him, considering he's been able to make me feel more than I thought I was capable to. This pull he has on me most likely developed after I disappeared and the more I checked up on him, the stronger his hold became.

In the midst of my reflection, the pressure returns, knocking the metaphorical wind out of me. Forcing through the intensity, I frantically scan my surroundings to see what has happened and I realize Kian and that girl had abruptly rounded a corner and I had fallen far behind them.

"Damnit Kian slow down, you're killing me here!" I shout, mostly to myself and momentarily forgetting he can hear me. I am just as shocked as he is when he nearly jumps out of his shoes and turns to face me, wide-eyed.

"Maeve?!" he says barely believing I'm standing just half a street away from him.

Before I can return his brilliant declaration of my name with a sarcastic comment, feeling peeved from the sudden onset of pain, Giselle literally steps between us. "Kian? Who are you talking to?" her voice tinged with an annoying coquettish whisp.

My face contorts into a scowl as I stare at the back of her head. "None of your business bitc-"

Kian cuts me off. "Oh! No one, sorry. I thought I heard someone call me…" he replies. All of us look at the barely populated street, the only people present being those late for work and couldn't care less about two highschool students. I can't help but raise my brow at him and his unfortunate inability to keep it cool.

"Okay, well we should keep going if we don't want to be late," she says.

"Wow, not too bright," I say and this causes Kian to give me a look. I shrug back. He can tell me to be nice all he wants, but if I was alive I would say the same damn thing.

"Actually Giselle, I realized I have something to do today so I'm not going right to school, but I can walk you the rest of the way if you'd like?" he offers and I pray this idiotic girl says no.

"Oh, umm… no go ahead. I don't want to keep you. See you at practice later?" she questions.

He nods and waves his goodbye as he walks back this way, passing me for show. I follow him, starting to feel, for a brief moment, like the love-struck puppy myself. "Where the hell have you been? I haven't stopped thinking about you since last time!" he shouts as soon as Giselle is too far away to be a bother.

"Avoiding your painful summons," I cooly snap back at him, only glancing over to see his reaction.

"My what?" he questions, his tone sharp yet confused.

"It's a theory, but I think every time you are thinking of me, you create this unconscious energy that summons me. The result being this odd suffocating pressure." I can see the wheels turning in his brain as his eyes dart from me to the cobbled street to the buildings around us.

When the fog dissipates and he comes back to reality, he simply shrugs. "Well, at least I know how to get in contact with you. You know, in case you decide to disappear again."

I stare at him for a moment, showing nothing on my face. It doesn't bother me that he doesn't dwell on this. I mean, I'm dead, not much bothers me now a-days. "I was busy these last two months so I didn't have time to come and see you," I lie. I *was* busy looking for my killer, but I *did* have the opportunity to see him and I did a few times, without his knowledge. Of course, the fact that I did find the time to check up on him has been this major distraction and the thing that forced me to insert myself into his life again.

I can tell he doesn't believe me, but he lets it go. Redirecting he brings us back the original question, "do you want me to help you with your humanity? I don't want or need to waste my time helping you if you don't care." He lays down this ultimatum with confidence in his voice, but I can see the worry behind his beautiful eyes and the lines smoothing his sharp square features. I feel the pit in my stomach grow. He doesn't want me to leave and frankly I don't either, but it would be easier, if not for me, than for him.

"Fine I'm in," I say and when his glare hardens I huff and continue. "And, I won't disappear for long stretches of time from now on," I state, raising my brows sarcastically asking if that's enough.

"And if I call you, you'll come?" he pushes and I scoff.

"I'm not a dog, Kian."

His ears reddened and he scratches the back of his neck uncomfortably, but I find myself forgetting his accidental insult as my eyes are drawn to his rippling muscles. He really is a beautiful boy. *This could be fun*, I think to myself. As time starts to drag with neither of us speaking a word I cough to bring us both back to reality.

"Why don't you go back to school? I don't want you too invested in my humanity that you neglect your human responsibilities," I state. He looks down at me suspiciously and I roll my silver eyes. "I won't run away."

It takes him a moment, but he is satisfied with my blatant assurance and walks away. I stay put and it's a good thing I did because a few times Kian looks back at me to make sure I'm still there and haven't disappeared into a ghostly mist. I wiggle my fingers at him in a little wave before he makes his final turn away from me and disappears inside the gates of the school, which apparently was close this whole time.

I spend the day wandering the wintry market that is set up almost every day, watching the elderly that populates it enjoy their blissful aging. Their happiness bothers me, as though their wrinkled faces, grey hair and creaky bones are better than my immortally translucent, alabaster skin and faded black hair. Suddenly, my face twists into a scowl as a dyed-blonde woman with blue, wise eyes passes me, unknowing of her insult to my existence.

She's in the realm of thirty-eight or forty, the age I would be had I not been murdered twenty years ago. I find myself following her, intrigued by my offense to her. I've never thought about my death in this manner before. The hatred I've felt always came from my desire to kill my killer, but this... this loathing is coming from nothing other than jealousy. I was deprived of many of the natural things this woman got. Unlike her, I can't age, I can't grow my wisdom through my life experiences. I'm practically stuck in every way as the eighteen-year-old girl I died as. I know there's no point dwelling on the unfairness of it all and with Kian helping me maybe I can get something out of this. I may talk a big game, but I really do want my humanity back. I'm just... scared.

I'm scared when he finds out what I've truly become, he'll run away and leave me to succumb to my eternal loneliness. I'm afraid that I'll lose myself to his promises and set myself up with hopes and wishes that will never come true. And, I'm afraid I won't get my revenge, no matter what form it may take. Shaking my head of such universally damning thoughts, I wait, perched on the ledge of the cement gate that surrounds the school. The height offering a visual vantage point not generally available to me. I suppose it was an unnecessary struggle, scaling the wall, as I watch the horde of students feed out of the building and Kian is all but towering above them.

Suddenly, that familiar "pressure" envelopes my body and I curl over, groaning in ghostly echoes. "I'm right here!" I shout in pain so Kian will stop that supernatural pull on me. He jumps like a frightened cat and within moments the compulsion is gone and I am left with only that dead nothingness.

"Maeve! I'm sorry! I didn't see you there!" he apologizes pushing his way through curious onlookers. He seems to notice their peculiar expression and hurriedly pulls out his phone as if there is someone on the other end. Rather that than talking to an invisible ghost perched on the wall above him.

I don't reply, I just jump down from my ledge and land fluidly on the snow-coated ground. "Let's get to retrieving my humanity. You've had ten hours to come up with a strategy, so I'm expecting a lot," the sarcasm in my voice is a rebellion to the hope that I might feel something more than pain and emptiness. He nods meekly, trying not to cause me any more pain as he beckons me closer. Despite his attempts, the pressure returns, although a little duller than usual. "I should figure out a way to counteract the effect of your calling!" I worry for a moment that my flippant attitude has started to bother him as I see the way his mouth draws down and his brows furrow. Even angry he's beautiful, but I don't let that distract me. "So, what *did* you come up with?"

The question rings in the air between us for a moment, and as though I spoke the magic words, snow begins to fall from the sky, dusting us with little fairy kisses. He turns from me and stares into the sprinkling snow. "It's not snowing too hard, so I thought we could go skating," he says nonchalantly.

"Look, I'm sorry if I was rude, I suppose my knack for communicating with others has diminished these past few years." Kian doesn't respond, so I glance over at him. He looks as if he's thinking about something else. His eyes are clouded and his energy feels distant. "You look troubled. Would you care to share why that is?" I offer.

Finally, he smiles at me gratefully, but there is darkness behind his eyes. "It's nothing really. Why don't we keep going." Although when he says this, I can tell deep in his voice he's not really trying to convince me. Directing me away from the matter, we continue towards our destination, him mentioning that we shouldn't be too far by now. I don't push the matter with him. This guy has only known me for three months and even with that time, we barely took any of it to get to know one another.

We arrive at the outdoor skating rink, the snowfall managing to keep other people away. So, we decide to take full advantage of it ourselves. It takes Kian a minute to put on the proper footwear, making me laugh when he stumbles over asking me if I need help with mine. Quickly he back-tracks as he recalls I'm a "ghost" and we both share a moment to laugh on his clumsy recollection. Something in me flutters as we look into each other's eyes, sharing a brief moment to laugh at my unfortunate situation. It's a new feeling, that's hard to describe, but I don't let it distract me too much from the rest of the day.

When we step from the sugared snow onto the thinly-coated ice, Kian takes off on a lap around the rink. He checks the surface for land mines, piles of snow or broken ice. While he does this, I stare down at my pale, translucent feet. I've never tried anything like this before, skating without a body to hold me up or get hurt if I fall. I don't feel the thrill of the cold air bitting my cheeks, and I miss the rosy flush that should follow but doesn't. I miss the battle of the wind tugging at my long dark hair and the urge to tie it up quickly before it tangles. But most of all, I miss the feeling of holding on, to whomever was with me, our skin frozen to the touch, and yet still humming with life.

"Maeve! You should try skating a bit. I don't know how it works for you, but I'm sure once we figure it out, you could have some fun!" Kian shouts as he passes me once more. His speed drags me into the wind and causes me to fly forward as though I was skating behind him. "Wow! That was quick! How are you doing that?" he calls incredulously.

"I don't know..." I mutter, amazed as I glide gracefully in the wind behind him. "I think... I think the wind is acting as my skates," I wonder.

"Amazing!" he says back, his unnecessarily handsome features molding into child-like expressions of glee.

I trail behind him but my mind questions if it's possible for me to increase my speed. How I can become the air around him and potentially skate by his side. At a moment like this, I would breath out, an old habit that would calm my nerves. But instead, I simply invoke my supernatural connection with the earth. I ask the wind to lift me and slowly it does, pulling me over to Kian's side. I can't help but giggle with glee. In my high, I look over at Kian, proud of what I was accomplishing, and if I could blush I would have. I find him staring at me with such a passionate expression, I can't describe it.

"What?" I ask, my voice soft and frail like the whispering gust around us.

He doesn't even blink before he responds. "I've never seen anyone like you before."

I look away. "You mean a dead girl?" I joke in an attempt to lighten the intensity. Everything seems to be moving too quickly now as the fluttery feeling I had earlier comes back. I start to wonder if he feels it too and as I gaze into his smoldering eyes, I'm sure he has to.

"Sure," is all Kian says and though I know there is more, once again, I let it be. I can't let him draw me in, no matter how he intrigues me or how right it feels to be here with him. Not only are we from different times, I mean for god's sake! I would be thirty-eight if I was alive! But I am also dead, and as I'm sure I've mentioned before, it doesn't really work out for souls from different places. We decide it's time to put up the skates and take a walk and as Kian ties the laces of his shoes together I decided to break the silence.

"So, tell me about you," I say. I can at least get to know him better.

He doesn't respond quite yet, as though I surprised him out of his thoughts. "Well," he starts. "I live with my dad near the highschool and my mom left years ago."

"I'm sorry to hear about your mom, but are you close with your dad?"

He shrugs. "Ya, we are pretty close. He works a lot so it's nice when I do get to see him and he always makes up for his absences by going to my football games and academic awards and such," he explains. His mood seems to lighten as he talks about his father and that puts me at ease. "What about you and your family?" he asks and I smile despondently.

Since my death I avoid thinking about my parents. It makes me want to see them and I almost destroyed half the city the first and last time I visited. It was the day after I became this phantom. I stop short, silent. Based of my sudden retreat, Kian acknowledges my agony.

"I'm sorry that I brought it up, you don't have to say anything if you're not comfortable with it."

Shaking my head, I confess my thoughts. "It's alright, I just haven't thought about them in a while."

"I see. I guess that makes sense." He sounds almost humbled when I decide to open up to him.

"Anyways, I suppose they are doing okay. I haven't seen them in a while. The last time I saw them they were grieving my death." I stop for a moment, remembering. "Though... I did hear something a while back that they had decided against getting a divorce and a couple of years after that, they moved back to Colorado."

"It must feel nice that they were able to stay together," he says compassionately. "What about siblings?"

"I was an only child. I remember my parents always talking about wanting another kid, but they never got the chance after what happened."

He nods. "I'm an only child too."

Smiling at this thing we have in common, I continue. "I had a better relationship with my mom than dad, he was always working and she made time for me between her writing and her painting. At times I would help her." Nostalgia taking over, I think back to the crystal clear memories of laying on the floor with mom playing cards, board games, reading, and more. My dad holed away in his office working diligently until we would sneak in and tickle him out of his efficient stupor. I hold myself a bit bigger, removing myself from the heavy emotions taking over. "Outside of all of this, this humanity business and what not, I really miss my family."

"Maeve?" Kian nearly whispers, his body tensed so he won't move and startle me.

"I'm okay," I reassure, mainly towards myself. Taking a moment to collect my thoughts I focus on the present once again. "So, what's the next step in your great plan?" I tease him and he chuckles tentatively.

"Honestly, the skating was as far as I got today," he confesses, his ears turning a humble shade of red.

I shrug. "Hey that's alright. I think we made some progress today."

"Oh ya?" he teases back, his eyes flashing a darker shade of blue when they meet mine. I quickly look away, not expecting the rush of passion I feel within moments. It should be illegal for him to be this pretty.

We realize after we have been walking around aimlessly for a while, that we were practically ignoring each other, so we decide it's time for us to go our separate ways for the evening. I offer to walk him home, though I'm not quite sure why. Of course, setting a new destination doesn't rectify the silence that had consumed us, and neither of us were taking any steps to rectify that. That is, until I feel his eyes bearing through me and I look to my right, interested in what he wants.

"What is it this time?" I tease him, folding my hands behind my back.

He shakes his head. "Nothing, I'm just looking at you," he responds bluntly.

"Like what you see?" To further my point, I offer a sarcastic pose. I feel a coat of panic wrap around my shoulders when he doesn't respond. Waiting a couple more seconds, I come to the uncomfortable conclusion that he really isn't going to say anything. "Earth to Kian," I mock, almost immediately regretting it as I realize I don't actually want to hear his answer, whichever way it might have gone.

"Sorry, got lost in thought," he says vaguely and I'm grateful because that means he is going to ignore my taunting.

"I think you're the first guy I've met who thinks this much," I think aloud. He chuckles as a response and I'm glad for that. Once again, we fall back into our famous silence. This time though, it doesn't feel all-consuming as it had last time, it feels comfortable, natural.

CHAPTER

4

I've gone back and forth between visiting Kian when I'm called and continuing the search for my killer. As of yet I have no luck with the latter. I notice how much closer the two of us have gotten and a part of me worries we might be getting too close.

"So what are we?" Kian questions, his blank tone pulling me curiously out of my thoughts.

"What do you mean?" I return coyly.

"I mean can I call you a friend? Or is that possible since you're a ghost?" he says, a deep chuckle in his throat.

"Oh, I suppose friends are fine," I answer, feeling the tension that had stabbed like barbs through the air dissipate.

"What did you think I meant?" he laughs and fakes a playful nudge at me.

"Nothing. Friends are good," I shrug. My intangible body flushes hot, embarrassed, before reverting back to nothingness.

Nodding resolutely, Kian holds out his hand to me. "We already know we can touch, so shaking hands to make our new friendship official shouldn't be a problem," he argues, sorting out the reasoning in his head for this display.

"Alright…" I say cautiously as I reach my hand towards him. Impatient with how long I was taking, he shoots his out and grabs ahold of mine. I flinch at the suddenness of our contact, but take a moment to register how it feels to touch him.

Unsurprisingly, I can't exactly feel his living flesh, but I can feel the nervous energy surrounding it, as though his soul is living as a coat around the outside of his body. The longer we hold onto each other the more I develop a resolute understanding of what he's feeling at this moment. I try not to overthink the strange combination of sadness, joy, and passion rolling into me like wind-blown waves. As his emotions are becoming more concrete I feel a strange, frightening sensation growing inside me.

"Kian… something is happening!" I yelp, horrified as I feel myself uncontrollably melting away.

His face turns from the calmed satisfaction that was previously displayed to wide-eyed terror. "What?" he says, his tone presenting itself as though that single word will stop whatever is going on. Suddenly, he looks down at my feet and he pulls me in. "Maeve what's happening?" he shouts fretfully.

Before I can say a word, I am sucked into a familiar nothing. Not even a sound is heard as I lay motionless on the absent floor. I immediately recognize this void as the one I had appeared in last time and I feel the sudden urge to look for that blinding angelic light. I hear a mystic harmony of voices calling out to me once more, and I am swarmed with deja vu. Finally, I stand and ask it my burning question.

"Why does this keep happening to me?" my voice straining through the air to reach whoever might hear. I didn't expect an answer but, as I walk towards the light, it comes anyways.

"That is not for us to answer," the manifested mediums state vaguely. The sound is like a chorus of beautifully cultured voices that penetrate a sense of relief and a feeling that I am not entirely alone.

"How do I get back?" Though, as I'm asking this, I'm not quite sure I even want to go "back". Suddenly, my attention is drawn away from the anticipation of another vague answer. I feel a strange electric tingling in my fingers, causing me to look down. In shock I watch my visible yet intangible form vanishing in front of my eyes. I stop my progression towards the all-consuming light and its chorus of companionship. As soon as I do, the vanishing halts as well. I raise an inquisitive brow and decide I need to experiment with this phenomenon. I feel a new desire to shape my understanding of this power they have to shift my form. Taking difficult steps away from the angelic light, I watch in awe as my form regenerates the further away I am from the white nothingness. Every step I take comes easier as I resist its longing pull of peacefulness.

"Maeve, Maeve come to us. It is time, you know it is time," the voices call, synchronized in their pleasantness but with an air of despair.

I continue to resist their callings, though I feel an overwhelming sense of lament. I retreat from the veiled portal of their control and persuasion. Their chorus fills my ears, urging me to stay with them and to be at peace. But I can't leave yet, I haven't completed my mission.

"I'm sorry! I can't!" I scream. What about Kian… thoughts of him rush through my head, blocking the howling of the voices. All at once, everything seems to fall in on me and I collapse, numb and dazed. In what might have been just a few moments, I wake in the arms of the boy whose face never left my thoughts as I fought to leave that peaceful light.

"Maeve?" he says, his voice soft and broken with concern.

"I'm fine," I say. My tone rebounds loudly in our ears, causing us to flinch in unison.

"Where did you go again?" he asks, but his eyes tell me he doesn't actually want to know.

"I-" I'm cut off from my response as I look down and see the familiar glow of my skin as it is in contact with his.

Again, a realization hits me. I think back to the last time we had such intimate contact. The longer Kian holds onto me the sensation of losing myself starts again and I feel myself being engulfed once more. Realization hits me suddenly, like the back of an angry hand. "Kian, let go of me," I say, my voice desperate.

"What? No, you just disappeared and now that I have you again you want me to let you go? No I can't do that," he rambles, anxiety tensing his body as he holds onto me.

"That's exactly why I disappeared!" I yell. "Now let go of me before it happens again!" I flinch at my harshness and the distraught way Kian's face falls when he hears this.

"It's my fault?" he questions and I see the past and present events playing like a projected movie against his eyes.

I shake my head. "That's not what I meant. I just mean that... well... we are two different beings. We knew we were testing the bounds of the natural and the supernatural. This shouldn't be so much of a shock..." I stutter, trying to convince him to come back to me as he is off in his own world of despair. "Kian, it's alright, neither of us knew what the consequences of us being friends would be, just that there are some."

At this, he looks up at me. His gorgeous blue eyes boring into mine, making sure I am truly alright with this. "Then it's decided, I won't touch you again. But I can't stay away from you," he states, the switch between the vulnerable boy I saw a moment ago and the confident one now gives me whiplash.

I take a moment before responding, contemplating whether or not what I am about to say is feasible, all the while knowing it could be misinterpreted. I proceed anyway, cautious in my delivery. "I absolutely don't want you to stay away from me." Ignoring the shock that veils his face, I continue. "I did at first because I thought you would disrupt my plan for vengeance, but something about you intrigues me and I've realized that even if you could leave me now, I couldn't leave you."

"Don't get me wrong… I'm honestly quite terrified of going back to that void, the place I disappear to every time we touch. But I… I think I'm willing to risk it again for you."

"So, what does this mean?" Kian asks and I see a recognizable flare of hope in his eyes.

Though I hold that hope too, I realize the danger we'd be putting ourselves in, besides we have barely even become friends and I can't risk breaking whatever we have for more fragile uncertainty. "It means… we are friends and you promised to help me get my humanity back," I state, lying through my teeth.

"Right. I can't break a promise to a *ghost* now can I?" he says, annoyance and rejection lining his silver tongue.

"Right." The pure hurt I feel at his classification of me shocks me into near silence.

I had never had a problem with being this apparition before now, before him, and I simply don't know how to react to it. Part of me believed he had seen more than the mockingly-intangible being I am. But I suppose I put too much faith in a living person who couldn't understand the rage and destruction that engulfed me the moment that man took my life. *I've been distracted from my mission and I can't let that happen again,* I think to myself as I trail behind Kian. At some point when I was lost in thought we had started walking again.

"Where are we going?" I ask now that I am fully aware of the fact that we are moving again.

"Well, since I'm stuck with you, on to my next step in the Re-Humanization Plan," he responds flatly. His dull demeanor shocks me into a silent annoyance for a while, as we all but drag our feet through the snow.

"Let's get a move on then," I state with a feigned sugary-sweet tone. To emphasize my point, I add a little spring to my step, look back at him once I've gone a good few paces ahead, and tilt my head, nearly gracing him with a little wink.

"What are you doing?" he asks and I can hear the restrained laugh in his tone.

He can't resist my teasing. He never could, I think, slightly biting my lower lip to keep from grinning too widely. "Nothing, just trying to be excited about this plan of yours!" At this, he can't help but join in my teasing and frolicking and we dance around each other in the empty, snow-laden street. Despite all the laughter, I still notice only one of us leaving footprints on the otherwise undisturbed white blanket below.

Suddenly, a crystal flake falls from the sky and dances like a fairy in front of my eyes. It then cascades gracefully, joining its kin in repairing the disturbed ground.

"Kian...!" I whisper as if speaking any louder would frighten the fragile beauties away.

"Snowflakes," he whispers back. I roll my eyes and give him the *'duh, I know they are snowflakes'* look before focusing back on their gentle waltz in air. Walking towards me, he stands with his back against mine, leaving enough room so we wouldn't be tempted to touch. The snowflakes float about us, offering to heal our scars with their cool tickles. As expected, the flakes drift through me as though I am vapor until the wind picks me up, lifts me into the air, and I dance with them. It almost feels as though I've become one myself.

"Maeve!" Kian shouts incredulously, watching in awe as I drift about, dancing on the gentle breeze amongst the snowflakes. A welcomed friend amongst them.

With a new vantage point, I look down at him. His sandy blonde hair is sprinkled with fluffy snowflakes, his crystal blue eyes exotically bright in the reflection of the white snow. He is so spectacular I am forced to wonder which one of us is actually supernatural. His tan skin flushes in the cold. But I see no flawed display in this, instead it's almost as if the blood rushing to warm his cheeks offers a real youthfulness. I am jealous of him and this simple livelihood that I no longer possess. Shaking my thoughts away from that, I focus instead on how amazing he looks. Staring at him now, I wonder if he could be the only person who's beauty rivals that of God. Metaphorically speaking.

"Come down from there." His voice is husky and raw, probably from the intense cold that seems to be affecting him now.

"Yeah. We should get you inside." I mentally urge the wind to set me on my feet again, which it politely does. "Let's go to a cafe and get you something warm to drink," I offer, as I notice a shiver wrack his body.

Nodding his approval, we set off in search of a comfy place to sit that isn't too crowded on this sunday afternoon. Luckily, we quickly find one that is empty outside of a few stragglers, too busy reading their books to chitchat or notice Kian talking to himself.

"I'll find a table, go get something to warm yourself," I say, motioning with my outstretched arm to the counter where the barista looks at him like *he's* the hot cup of coffee. It makes me grit my teeth, something I used to do before whenever I was extremely jealous. I already knew I had some strange attraction to this boy, but I didn't really expect it to cause a reflective action, especially one from before I died.

"Okay, be back in a second," he says, a little breathless from our trek through the snow.

Nodding my response, I turned away from him and looked around the cafe. It's cute and has a familiarity about it, like it was some place I might have visited when I was alive. Spotting an empty booth in a darker corner of the place, and deciding it will serve to our special requirements, I make my way towards it. Taking a seat, I look back to Kian to check his progress and instead I catch this average, red-haired barista shamelessly flirting with him. I scowl and glance away from them. I cannot allow myself the freedom of being annoyed with him. Not when it comes to invading his privacy or disrupting normal life things.

I hum to myself while I wait and stare at the snow dancing gleefully outside the frosted window. I sigh noticing the fact that my breath does not fog up the glass as it would with anyone else in the coffee shop. It's like in one moment, I feel a sense of humanity returning and in the next I am reminded of my current state. The reality being, I'm just a ghost. Clearing my throat, I continue my tune for what feels like an entire song before Kian comes and takes his saved seat.

"What are you looking at?" he says, interrupting my melody with his deep tone.

"Nothing," I state, not turning to meet his eyes. If I did I would confront him about talking to the other girl even though I know that it is not my place to do so. "Did you get a coffee?" I ask, trying to make small talk to rid my brain of the constant image of the two of them. *I mean come on Maeve! They were just talking!*

"Yeah." A brief moment of silence passes between us. "Maeve, are you alright?" Kian finally asks and when I look at him, he has his brows furrowed and his lips pressed together.

"No, but it's personal," I shrug. I know I can't lie to him so I go the route of vaguity. And he catches on.

"Okay, I won't push," he teases and takes a sip of his hot coffee. The steam gives a slight shimmer to his skin and turns his face rosey. I watch him savor the cup of liquid gold and realize how much I miss the slightly bitter taste, of not just coffee, but of life.

"Excuse me." Out of the blue, I abruptly leave the table and in his shock Kian spills some of the steaming brown liquid on his hand.

"Damn!" he curses, setting down the mug and scraping the napkin across his hand as though that will get rid of the burn.

"Oh... um okay. Don't go too far," he attempts a joke, but it's lost in his eyes because instead all I see the pain from the burn.

I walk about the cafe, not knowing exactly what I am looking for, but sensing that I will find something important. Following along the four walls, which have obviously been recently remodeled, I study the old pictures, the collage of news clippings, the magazine articles, and even inspect the childrens' drawings. Something about this place is familiar and my phantomed body is pulled into searching for the why.

I trek through the restaurant, unbothered by the customers who seem to be unaware of me anyways. I stare heartily at the photographs pinned to the freshly painted soft yellow walls. When I come across a hand-made maroon frame, I stop and my mouth all but falls to the floor in bewilderment. There, in the picture, is my face, alive and brimming with excitement, my parents smiling down at me in their usual respectful and proud manner. I rest my hand on the glass barrier between me and my living reflection, struck by this beautiful moment captured in time that lives on despite how I am now stuck in this in between.

"Maeve, you've been staring at that picture for ten minutes now, what…" Kian's words drift into nothingness as he takes a closer look at the black and white photograph of me and my parents in a historic version of this cafe. "Is… is that you?" he spits the words out, with much difficulty due to his surprise. It seems to cause him to choke on his recently sipped coffee.

"Yes… I-I think this is my eighteenth birthday…" I wonder, too entranced by what I used to be.

"You were beautiful."

"I was, wasn't I?" I reply, not an ounce of conceit in my tone. I suppose it can take death for a girl to realize how great she is… was.

"You look a lot like your mother," he says, pointing to her, she's the mere representation of what I might look like now had I still been alive.

Deciding to share just a bit of information with him, I force my eyes away from my family and look at the boy to my side. "My mom's about thirty-nine in this picture, a year older than I would've been right now," I say, sadness coating my voice thickly as the realization that I will never look older and wiser, as my mother did in the picture.

Kian says nothing, respecting my silent wish to absorb this moment and process the memories that overcome me. I try to retain some semblance of the refined girl I used to be. Flashes of birthdays in Colorado, picnics over summer vacations, and going to movies with friends. Then we moved here to Michigan and the moments that lead up to that picture. I had just received my acceptance letter to the college of my dreams and on the day of my birthday! My parents were so proud they took me out for a special treat and told everyone in the cafe of my amazing news. The owner of the cafe, back when it was a family-run business, asked to take our picture and hang it on the wall as a momento. It truly was the best birthday. How was I to know all that joy and excitement was to end just a few weeks later when I was murdered.

"We should go," I state suddenly, the cause for this known only by me.

"Are you sure? Is everything okay?" Kian asks. I can see him questioning himself about why he didn't say something more to help whatever inner turmoil I was going through.

I feel myself losing the semblance of control i've had to this point. "Everything won't be fine in a minute, so I suggest we leave," I reply as quickly and as calmly as I can. I can feel an overwhelming emotion trying to claw its way out of my phantasmic form. I've avoided using this strange, almost too powerful, connection with nature for the past twenty years. Since my death, I have had this ability to full immense energy from the wind, water, light, and even sometimes manipulate people with such force that I could destroy whole cities with a single natural disaster. It's not a power I conceitedly ignore, I respect the turmoil and damage it can cause if I can't control it.

Kian sees the seriousness of the situation in my eyes and with swift strides he leaves his cup behind and grabs his wallet. As he does this, a paper falls out from the leather pocket and drifts tauntingly onto the table. I can tell what it is, even before it lands face up. The numbers on the page glare at me mockingly. It adds to my increasingly uncontrollable emotion that has begun to chill the room and fog the glass windows, so thick that no one can see outside.

I watch with focused eyes as he reaches out and grabs the paper, his hand moving like a striking serpent. After he has brought it back into his possession, I am shocked into complete tranquility when his hand flexes and he crumples it in his palm, tossing it resolutely into the trash bin. "Wasn't that something important?" I ask, unable to refrain from asking the question even though in the moment, I want to maintain my unfeeling sense, I need to know if he really wanted that girl's number.

"You saw that huh?" he says, rubbing the back of his neck embarrassed. "Uh, it was a sweet gesture and all, but I just wasn't interested in her," he explains. I can feel myself settling a little at his confirmation but I'm still not back to normal so I try to usher us outside faster. As we finally make it out of the cafe and I focus back on him, I'm relieved to see the earnestness in his captivating blue eyes. On the other hand, I'm also relieved that I haven't demolished the entire city. I realize I had been staring at him with a blank expression and I can feel how his nerves have grown.

I chuckle and find myself quickly reassuring him. "It's alright, I'm not going to blow up Michigan because of some girl's crush..." as I'm saying this, I realize that was actually a contributing factor to what I was going to do only moments ago.

"Right... no, yeah..." Kian stutters, his beautiful face scrunching in confusion at where he was going with that.

"Anyway, let's get you home. I have some ghostly wandering to do before the day is up and the sun goes down. I don't want to be late for that," I state, needing to distance myself from him, from this, from everything.

"Okay, sure," he nods and we start another trek through the snow. It doesn't take us long to get back to his house and I leave him with a wave at the front door, my escape in sight. He turns away and jingles his keys into the lock on the wooden door and I watch for a moment. I know I should hurry and leave, but I'm afraid if I do, I won't come back. This suffocating feeling might actually be enough to keep me away. "Hey, Maeve..." I hear Kian say and I feel the wind hurry and lift me away when I start to panic. I fix my fleeting gaze on his drawn expression and defeated pose and am shocked numb when the air that pulls me away betrays me and carries his passionate whispers to my ears. *"Please come back..."*

CHAPTER

5

B y the time my wandering has started to drift away and my mind's haze clears along with it, it's nearing midnight and the moon smiles down like that of a cheshire cat. Unbothered by the frigid air or the mystery that hides in the darkness, I walk the path of a small lake to a waterside bench. There I watch the waves crack against each other in a riotous, yet peaceful, dance. There is an unmistakable glow to the city tonight and it leads me willingly into the waves' dance, an eerie and rightfully mystical picture. My faded raven hair doesn't catch the light as it used to, but instead, it fans into the midnight and becomes a part of it. My pale, translucent skin glowing like the moon as my feet touch soundlessly to the pavement in graceful bounds, twirls, and sashays.

A long buried memory slowly greets my remembrance as I dance into it, consuming myself with it. *Alive, I am in the arms* of one of my fathers' friends' sons. We are in a room. I study it curiously, trying to remember where we were. Despite my intense glare at my surroundings, everything is uncommonly blurry, as though there is a veil of static surrounding everything but me and my dance partner.

"Miss Cowen?" the boy asserts, offended that my attention has drifted from him.

"Oh, my apologies Mr. Johnson, I seem to have been too taken by the night," I assure him. Mentally I am rolling my eyes at his pouty attitude. This child-like behavior is easily thwarted the moment he becomes the center of my attention again. He nods, embracing me tighter as we continue the dance. By the end of the song, which seems to go on for far too long in my opinion, I notice the spotlight is on us in the middle of a fuzzy grand hall. The fellow dancers displayed a familiar disappointed accusation of stealing their moment. Suddenly, the beam of fake moonlight becomes too much and I find myself ditching my date on the dance floor. Gasping for air, I search for a way out of this suffocating embrace of their posh attentions. Father catches me and pulls me into a comforting hug. It doubles as a secretive escape, and he leads me securely into the hallway.

"What's that matter, Pumpkin?" Dad asks, patting my hair as I nuzzle my face further into his broad, warm chest.

"I don't like these parties. All these people want attention or something from you. It's suffocating," I confide in him as my breathing returns to normal.

"I know how you feel, but sometimes we have to deal with people we don't approve of. We don't have to like them, and we shouldn't expend too much of our energy on them, but we do have to be tolerant."

Nodding as I consider his words, I think out loud. "I think I can do that. There's no law saying I have to be like them."

Dad shrugs, "See you're getting it. And besides, saying you're anything like the guests we have out there would be the biggest lie anyone has ever told." With a parental smirk and one last pat on my head, he gently pushes me away. Holding onto my shoulders, he bends down enough to meet my eyes. "I think you're ready to go back, yes?"

As my father and I return to the party, the memory fades. I am left standing in the middle of this Michigan park wishing I could cry to release the tension trapped in me by these human sentiments. This mixture of sadness, love, and joy are sometimes too intense and it feels like I am being torn apart by them. This form not being suited to maintain the power of them. This time, I am shocked to find the wind hasn't stirred and nothing lays in ruins. Usually every time I feel this way, nature picks up on it and expresses my turmoil for me.

Again the words of my father ring in my ears, *I think you're ready to.* Back then he was telling me to go back into the party, but where should I go back this time? I'm not at a business event with my parents, or ditching school with friends. I'm a dead girl standing alone in the dark. *Wait*, I think to myself, *I'm not alone anymore. Someone has seen me, someone has vowed to stay by my side… and I tried to push him away for it.* "Kian," I state and the moment I do, realization hits me like I am plummeting off of a cliff. Life is too short, for him, to avoid these feelings, and maybe the fact that I'm not suppressing them anymore is keeping this world intact. Our world intact.

If he'll take me, with all my supernatural baggage, why let the fact that I'm dead stand in the way of what I've been feeling since the moment he threw himself in front of a car for me. I know it hasn't been long since that day, but the memories swirling in my head of ice skating and long talks, cafes and walks in the snow, makes me feel like I've known him forever. The connection we share from the bond of our souls, to when we touch causing many unexplainable things to happen, were all signs informing us, sometimes ungracefully, that the next choice I have to make has been an inevitable one. "I'm ready to go back to him."

I take off through the night, too focused to worry about running through trees and posts and stray cats. My black hair snapping and wiping behind me, like the cape of a hero on a mission. When I make it to the house, it's well past two in the morning, but this isn't something that can wait. Unashamed, I scale the side of his house and force myself through the inorganic mess of his window, offering myself a stable landing on his carpeted floor.

"Jesus!" Kian's deep voice yelps invisibly in the pitch black room. The aura of the tight enclosed space is shockingly similar to the void. That idea unnerves me to the point where my footsteps falter and I stand unmoving in the middle of his room. He can see me with the moon-like radiance that creeps in behind my figure. He is able to stumble through the darkness towards me until he stands close enough that the faint shimmer from my ghostly body dimly lights up his face. The shadows that surround his piercing blue eyes cause shivers to vibrate in the air around me. "Maeve?" he says, his voice disbelieving. "I thought you were never coming back."

Understanding that I am the cause of his lamentation breaks my heart and I bring my folded hands up to my chest, holding them there to distance myself from the pain my actions brought upon him. "I'm sorry," I whisper, my voice cracking with emotion. "I was planning on disappearing from your life, I thought that things would be easier... safer... if we kept away from each other. But I realize I can't forget you and you can't unsee me. Something changed that day when we met and if loving you destroys all universes as we know them, both yours and mine, then I'm willing to take that risk." Had I been alive, I'm sure I would be out of breath with the speed those words... no those revelations came pouring out of me.

Kian stays quiet. I feel like I've talked more now than I ever had when I was alive so I am silent too. It's strange that even though I'm near swimming in tension and overpowering emotion I don't feel like destroying everything in sight. The only reasoning I'm able to legitimize is that it has something to do with him, like he's subconsciously taking on everything my veil of a body cannot handle.

"I don't think I fully understand what you're asking of me," Kian says finally, his face not giving anything away.

My eyes bound away from him for a moment, formalizing the ultimate question in my head. I stutter over the words as I feel a crushing sadness wash over me, recognizing the certainty in his voice despite the question asked.

"I'm asking to stay by your side and I'm willing to accept the help you've offered. I want another chance," I beg. This is when the wind picks up on my grief and stirs into the room from crevices in the old house. I can see my grief mirrored in Kian's eyes, but they harden soon after, causing me to wonder if I actually saw it there.

"I did promise to help you in any way I can, but I can't let myself feel anything for you anymore.

I can't shake this feeling in the pit of my stomach that you are going to try and vanish again, and I don't think I could handle it." Kian takes a deep breath, not once looking away from me and facing his decision head-on.

Though I feel like crying I won't run away. This was his choice to make and it was always a possibility that I would be rejected. All I can ask of him is to be honest with me. And whatever his decision, I know I can still watch over him, even if I can't stand by his side. I wrack through the toiling thoughts in my brain, hoping sorting through them quickly might offer me some sort of relief. Soon enough the air around me starts to calm and I feel the weight of human emotions lifting off of my shoulders and drifting off with the wind. Slowly I remember how to shut off from this part of being human, something I did long ago when I realized it only caused destruction and pain for me. I think Kian notices my increasing veil of separation. He starts to reach for me, hesitates and pulls his hand back, almost disgusted with himself. As though securing the veil around myself, I do something I didn't know was possible and shut him out. Afterwards, I feel empty and dead again I look around the room, the fear of the void no longer exists as I compare the two places once more.

When my eyes find Kian, that supernatural bond, that used to pull me towards him is gone. The nothingness I feel doesn't waver in sadness. "I should let you get some sleep, I do remember humans needing to do menial things like that," I comment as I assuredly turn away from him and disappear out the window into the morning, still lacking the light of the sun. I wander the streets. Which becomes increasingly populated with the arrival of dawn, and the day continues its pattern of moving resolutely through time.

"Maybe it's about time I pick up where I left off on the search for my murderer," I say to myself. My blank eyes scan the world around me, unmoved by the twinkling of the suns rays on the wet grass of a park or made jealous by the giggling children on their way to school. I again remember how I gave up on the idea for a new life fifteen years ago. This revelation reminding me why exactly I did not want the promises Kian made in the first place. I find myself drifting back to this one particular memory of my short time in New Orleans.

—m—

Fifteen years ago.

I roamed the streets of New Orleans with solem curiosity, the supernatural elements of witches, voodoo and other deemed unholy crafts embedded into the city through years of history. It entices me. Part of me thought this place could give me answers to what I was, or maybe it was the gateway that would give me a second chance. Either a promise of another human life, or the chance to learn how to enact my revenge.

"I sense a disquieted soul nearby..." whispers the crackly voice of an accented woman. I turn to face whomever had spoken. The woman with unforgivingly wrinkled skin, black as coffee, was suddenly right beside me, so close that had I been human, I could have run right into her. She displayed a knowledge of despair in her golden eyes, as though she could see straight into me.

"Yes. There you are..." she says once again, her voice intense, yet welcoming.

"You see me?" my burning question is interrupted as she continues.

"Though, I cannot actually see you. My third eye can, hence my ability to sense your presence. What may I assist you with today? As I sense you have travelled a long way and fate has brought you into my path." I watch the woman for a moment, it peaks my interest that though she really can't see me, as she says, she can sense my "being".

I spend the next few weeks following this woman. She spoke of who she was and what she did, asked the universe why it needed her to help me. She tells me how she is a fourth generation, which at the time I didn't understand, and how she is passing her craft down to her grandchildren and her hopes that they will continue her legacy in helping stray souls like myself. She asked me questions too, questions that we both know I can't actually answer, at least in a way she can hear me. And yet, I found myself answering all her questions, intrigued by the living woman who had some strange connection with beings like myself. The last day I saw her was a special day in particular, because that was the day she finally answered one of my questions.

"You know dear, I have not yet mentioned it, but it is possible to bring the dead back to life, just not in the way everyone assumes..." here her voice fades out.

Part of me comes to the conclusion that she won't pick up again and I'll be left dangling on the empty hope brought by her words. That is until she sort of hops into the air - surprising considering her old age - and continues with her theory. "You can't get your same body back, it has long since deteriorated. However, with a willing person, and a witch like myself..." she chuckles in a grandmotherly way at this "...you can, in a sense, swap souls. The living person dies, only momentarily, but in that short time, your two souls with 'switch places' and with the old soul now out, your's is free to guide the body back to life."

I'm hanging on every word, even when she takes a moment to hurriedly gulp in a needed breath. "The only other time I have seen this happen, he hardly felt different, besides the being alive part." She laughs mischievously at this and I simply stare at her in shock.

"Of course, you must prepare as well. You can't expect them to do all the work. Your job would be to learn to fully rely on and trust the other person as they will be entrusting their body to you."

Once she says this I notice my excitement that had begun swirling the air around us into flouncing gusts, starts to dissipate. I was too hopeful for my own good, once again. Yeah, ask the murdered ghost with a revenge scheme to trust somebody. In the next moment I make a decision that I regret for the next fifteen years of my death, a decision made out of who can say. Guilt?

Disappointment? Fear? Either way, I left that day, leaving the woman to walk alone down the streets of a city I loved because, at the time, I felt like it was the only thing in my control. It was the only way I could pretend like I didn't just make the worst mistake of my death, well until the next day when I couldn't find her.

I looked everywhere for her, her home, the few streets she allowed herself to use, and her shop. Yet no matter where I went, it was like she had just vanished, disappeared off the face of the earth. I only stayed in Orleans for a little while after that, not able to bear the loss of that woman, the key to unlocking the door to humanity. It wasn't that we had become friends or anything. We couldn't actually speak and frankly, we never learned each others names. In reality it was more like she had become the physical representation of the first hope I had since my death. She was the first to show me the kindness and dispair of hope and I always expected her to be the last.

Present Day.

I snap out of the memory suddenly, as though it was drowning me and I was fighting for air, wrestling to be free of the evocation. I look around, unsure of where my wandering has taken me and trying to find the slightest bit familiarity in my surroundings. I feel a sinking in my gut as recognition of this place plows over me just like the car had twenty years ago, in this very spot. The air around me tightens and fury rips through the calm day, matching the fire raging in my soul. The ground starts to tremble as crisp pictures of the moment play in front of my eyes, inciting my hunger for revenge. I had successfully avoided this place since that day, knowing somewhere inside myself that if I came back, it would be the ruin of this city.

As I am looking around at the windblown chaos of people seeking shelter, my grey eyes all but meet the cold, unapologetic, and secretive ones I had looked up into so long ago. *I've found him!* He's older now, with broad shoulders and creases on his face that prove guilt, but not to the untrained eye. He walks steadily and with a power he has acquired over the years. The only satisfaction I get from looking at him, not dead, is the early-grey hair that scars the full snow blonde mass he has slicked back. I know I'm the main cause of that grey, the strain from killing me imprinted onto him and turning him into this false creature. Good. He deserves every possible pain and mutation before I kill him.

He can't see me, so I trail him a few blocks, plotting just how I might spend my energy ending him. I could blow down a building, crushing him flat. Or I could draw him into the street, placing him in the headlights of a sweet irony. As my vengeance boils over and I can hold myself back no longer, he conveniently walks into a corner shop, disappearing from sight. I choke on the scream ripped from my throat and the wind lashes about me. Now, people come face to face with my furry and scuffle out of the street so as not to be caught up in it. I force my way through the walls and shelves of the store to reach him, but my distraction resulted in his easy escape. My rage sends the wind flying through the store, knocking down rows of merchandise and the heavy wooden platforms they rested on. The shoppers all fall to their knees, covering their heads and any children from the onslaught of debri.

My torment follows me back into the street where it rattles cars and slings fallen bits of tree and bush into unsuspecting windows. Outside, I am no longer in pursuit, the walls of the building not forced to trap my rage. Everything ceases to crumble beneath my feet. After twenty years he's gone, again, and there is nothing I can do. With this dreaded understanding, I stand like a statue on the sidewalk, not really look at anything, just frozen in utter disbelief. It could be another twenty or even thirty years before I see him again. What if he dies in that time? What has this monster been capable of in his time here? Has he continued destroying life, having never paid for mine?

Abruptly, I fall into a maniacal laughing fit, crazed as I am suffocated by the idea that I may have just lost my only chance to fulfill my final wish, my burning desire. Once more I take stock in the loss of hope. I don't know what to do now. The boy I who I began to believe could bring me back to humanity doesn't think we are worth the risk. The woman who looked into my soul and offered me a taste of freedom from this revenge, I shunned. The man who murdered me just mocked my existential hatred with ignorance and self pity. And with all of that, I am still dead and I am still alone. I shake my head so as to help myself come down from my moment of insanity.

I wander back towards the park with the man-made pond in the center. I've always found that water calms me, stabilizes everything out of control, and sometimes, offers clips of memories that generally find some use in this meaningless after life. As I approach the crystalized pond, seemingly frozen in time with the frigid season, I'm rocked back by Kians voice protruding through the air into my head.

"I'm going to help you get your humanity back! Or... at least help you feel human again!"

And then the witches words.

"...it is possible to bring the dead back to life... with a willing person you can in a sense, switch souls..."

It's like the world around me dissolves and a blinding revelation of hopeful words echo boldly in my heart and bring a glimmer to my eyes. Could the two be connected? Is Kian my door to exiting this supernatural realm? Did it take me returning to this place of death to give me the road to peace? All I have truly known, up to this point, is that I wanted to kill the man who killed me. But once I met Kian, everything changed. The woman confirmed that in a way my spirit was still a form of existence and even with just that we can join one soul with another.

Maybe... just maybe... that is what love is too? Out of all of this... am I capable of falling in love and trusting another person? I used to only feel anger, hatred, or nothing at all, but now I feel more. Something more… human.

With this new mindset, I know what I have to do next. I'll take the next few months traveling back in time, back to where Kian and I spent our short lived existence together. I'll take this time to figure out how to make it up to him and make myself better for him. To prove that this is worth it and that I can commit to something good and not fall back into the hellhole of revenge.

The street where we met is unchanging despite the heavy traffic that tries to kneed our historic meeting out of the concrete. The outdoor ice rink with a fresh coat of snow, unbothered, atop the surface and reminding me of the unblemished promises made between the two of us. The wall of the school where I waited for him after discovering our bond and for a moment, allowing myself to wish that we hadn't let go of it. And then there's the cafe. The cafe where we went many times. It was the place I told him about my past and where the only evidence of me ever having been alive exists.

And that is where I find him. It's felt like forever since the last time my eyes fell upon this perfect person. Shockingly, I find him standing in front of the wall of pictures and if I could I know I would be feeling chocked up right about now. It's no coincidence that the final place on my path of repentance, leads me to him.

"Tell me something about when you were alive," he says suddenly. The sound of his voice makes me nearly swoon with a relaxed joy.

"I was always bad at apologizing," I reply, hoping my voice conveyed how much I loved him and how ready I was to make things right.

6

"My dad just got back into town so I will probably be spending more time out of the house. He is always mostly focused on work anyways," Kian comments blandly as we walk together through a park. Despite us making up a couple of weeks ago, things have still been pretty awkward between us and with the extra tension of his dad's return, it's been more difficult to get things back to normal between us. We still don't know exactly where we stand in each other's lives, but have mutually agreed to pick back up on our old promises and find a way to bring me back. The last part being a new addition to the promise after I had opened up to him about my time in time in New Orleans.

"Didn't he just come back from a trip?" I ask.

"Yeah, but when he's not traveling for the business, he's running it out of the fancy new office down the hill. So there's really no difference," he muses. It causes me to think back on my own father who's entire life was dedicated to his work, at least while I was alive.

"What kind of man is your father?" I ask, my curiosity a diversion to avoid thinking of my own family.

Kian shrugs. "He's broody and secretive. People who aren't his clients really don't seem to interest him. Occasionally though, he does his best attempt at the whole father-son bonding thing. Usually it turns out with us pretending to enjoy each other's presence and than getting bored of the act and going our separate ways."

"Do you look a lot like him?" I try to focus on his response, but his blonde hair, casually sweeping into his ocean eyes, tempts me with every blush of the wind against us to run my hands through it.

"Actually, he's always told me that I look more like my mother, with the blue eyes and sharp features. But I got his build and hair."

I nod, half listening. My eyes hungrily scanning him as though I haven't seen him in years. In all those months we were apart he has somehow become even more handsome and I'd bet all my inheritance (when I had an inheritance) that he has grown a bit too. In all the changes I can see in him, what is the most striking is the confidence he used to have has magnified into what I can only describe as maturity. It's quite fetching on him.

I crinkle my nose subconsciously, *Really Maeve, fetching?*

Suddenly, when I realize no one has said anything for a long time, I snap out of my stupor and crisply look away from him. I should be embarrassed, I know, I should feel ashamed that I am casing him so straightforwardly even after everything that happened, but I don't.

After we reunited we had a long conversation about where we are at with each other and I now have a clear understanding of where I stand with him and he knows where he stands with me. But despite the decision to maintain a platonic relationship through this process, I can't deny how I feel. I have struggled to remain respectful of our mutual decision, but damn it's hard when there is a flutter in the air that threatens to give me away whenever I'm near him or the heat that reaches deep into my cold illusion. Being so close to him just feels right, like he's the one who could finally give me everything I need. Everything, except the satisfaction of my vengeance, only to be content when my killer is dead.

Abruptly I bellow, in a not-so-casual way, "let's go do something!" We both know I do this as a desperate attempt to escape my thoughts, but in classic Kian fashion, he respectfully tries to ignore it.

"Uh, sure," he says, clearly still caught off-guard he forces himself to not draw attention to it. "What were you thinking?"

Realizing I have no followup plan, I shrug my shoulders in response. "We should do something besides walk aimlessly about Ann Arbor, as has become our repeated course of action."

"It has, hasn't it," he muses. "Let's see a movie! It's kinda cold today," he offers.

I don't have the heart to mindlessly muse over the human emotions conveyed on the big screen, but I have enough of a heart to not say no. I ultimately concede without rebuttal. "Okay, that sounds good." I grudgingly set off in the direction of the closest theatre. On arrival he buys one ticket, on popcorn, and one soda, to some science fiction movie that he doesn't even seem interested in. I can sense he thinks it will be full of enough action to distract us, sitting awkwardly close in a dark room together.

We meander through the red velvet hallways of the building searching for the lit up number four with the word *Arrival* spelled out in neon letters. When I was alive, coming to the movies was a treat, because I could escape into the imagination of the picture itself, and enjoy time with friends, get lost in the smell of salted, buttery popcorn and the soft whisper of carbonated fiz that tickled my nose. Senses, I regret the absence of. Walking through this place, humans would enjoy this explosion of nostalgia, but instead I am drawn to the hum of careless footsteps. They are taking this moment for granted. If I could cry, we'd be swimming in my cold, acidic, vengeful tears. I look at Kian, unaware of my current contemplation, wondering would he hold me? Console me like any other girl, if he knew the sorrow I felt in this moment?

"Maeve... are you alright?" he asks, there is a whimsical note of concern that loosens his tongue.

I nod with such urgency that I'm sure my neck would have snapped in two if it were capable. "Fine, I'm fine. Sorry. I got lost in thought for a moment there," I reassure him, feeling a flurry of something in my chest as his blue eyes darken with intention and focus entirely on me. "Let's go see the movie."

He seems hesitant to make a single move as though one step towards or away from me would spook me like a deer in headlights. So I walk past him into the gothic black room. The flicker of the large screen casts static shadows over the faces of the few people seated, engrossed in the trailers. As we take our own seats, I find myself feeling as though I have just been caught rummaging through something that I had no place digging into. How ironic that the thing I was looking for, the thing everyone believes is a basic human prerogative, is the exact thing that was taken unwillingly from the dead who want it the most.

A disturbed silence falls over the theatre, the only sounds coming from those devouring their treasured snacks and the heavy anticipation for the coming picture. Uncomfortably we sit in the plush chairs, though not because of the lumpy seats themselves or the awkward angles they rest at. We are too close, we both know that much. But there is nothing we can do about it now. I'm sure Kian doesn't want to make a scene, leaving abruptly. He must already be anxious, feeling questioning eyes on him as he sits there alone and seemingly talking to himself.

Acting as a repreve, the movie plays offering a mindless break from the attention I had on Kian. To be honest, my attention was mainly on Kian. I stare at him as though his face is the most engrossing movie I could ever see. I only look away when I feel that strange rumbling in my chest, like the weight of gravity has finally realized that I am still present on Earth and tries to bind me with force. Amused by this false power, I notice Kian shifting and as I turn to focus on him, we end up staring straight into each other's eyes, catching us both off guard.

"What are you doing?" he whispers and I can't decipher the tone of his voice considering his words were barely audible.

"Nothing, I was just looking," I reply, casually. My voice seems to boom though no one else but Kian can hear me.

He flinches and looks over at the others who are still enjoying the movie, ignorant as ever of the dead person in their presence. "Why?" he asks.

For once, I am able to decipher his mood and I'm not quite sure how to react. His question seemed harmless and maybe a little confused to find me staring. His tone begged for an answer, for a response he knows may not come.

Me, I'm waiting for, well I don't know. So we sit there. I drift back to when he confessed to me and the only thing I could think to do, was the absolute wrong thing. I ran off and disappeared. How can I blame him now for not understanding my feelings after all this time and all of the pretending since we've reunited. He must not be able to trust me, fearing I'm going to do what his mother did so long ago when she left him behind. Sadness wells up in me and I wish tears would come, just this once. He would then see how I feel right now. My eyes would show the tragedy of our reality, being from two separate worlds and how we can never fully understand the other person. Instead I have to settle for wasted words.

"I'm staring at you because I've fallen in love with you and there is nothing I can do to stop it."

Kian doesn't look surprised, but the familiar sadness and forced distance returns. "Maeve... you know-"

"Don't," I interrupt, holding my hand up between us, as though it could protect me from the rejection I was receiving. "This is my fault for always vanishing, too focused on my long time revenge scheme. Despite that, I clearly impacted you more than I ever had intended. But I need you to know that, now, I'm here for good." I notice how he flinches at the brief mention of murder and I feel the air tighten around me as though it's trying to choke the honesty from my throat. "I feel like I am constantly being punished. My life ripped from me, my vengeance left unfulfilled, and then I sabotage the first good thing that actually came my way. At first I couldn't feel anything and then you reminded me of the vast valley of human emotions beyond just hate, anger, and retribution. But I resisted, pushing you away because I was scared of the change." I pause for a second, keeping my gaze steady on him and preparing for what I have to say next.

"I don't understand what any of this means. Why you can see me and interact with me like you can. But I've come to the conclusion that I have to concede my fears and trust that it *is* for a reason. And, most of all, that I am destined to be with you."

"But you shouldn't... you shouldn't feel like you have to be with me just because of the stupid universe," he argues back and I nearly facepalm myself at his blatant lack of understanding.

"No, what I mean is, before you anything I did was meant to destroy everything around me because I was too damn angry at the world for letting this happen to me. Even now I'm angry. It kills me all over that people take advantage of everything they have simply because they are alive and have that choice! It infuriates me that I can't kill the man who took away my choice! But even worse, it kills me that the first person who treated me like I was still alive, like I still had my choice, doesn't trust me anymore. And because of what I did to him, he can't love me back."

Silence. Damned silence. It squeezes me in a suffocating embrace. The last words of my confession are a severe honesty that even baffles me. I don't condemn him for his contribution to the noiseless boundary between us. I mean what should I expect, I threw every ounce of my vulnerability at his feet. What is he to do with all of that? As these thoughts run through me, I find myself pleading into his perspicacious eyes and everything falls away as his perfect lips come crashing onto mine. In that moment I catch myself attempting to breathe but breathless, all I can manage is a gasp of utter disbelief.

I can't actually feel the warmth of his skin or his subconscious attempt to tuck my faded hair behind my ears. But to me, it is the perfect kiss. It's everything life is supposed to feel like and more. The longer his lips move with mine the more of his energy I feel pulsating into me like an organic heartbeat. I try to stay focused on feeling as much of him as I can, at this moment. It's like his rhythm is defibrillating my tormented heart back to life. Here and now I feel his livelihood through the core of my being. The pumping of his blood seems to warm my cold veins and the boiling energy that collides with my own in a shocking blast of existence. This sensation has evolved from when we first met. At first his touch was the opposite, it sent me into disarray like a violent tornado but now, it grounds me how gravity couldn't. It wasn't just a kiss, for a moment, I was alive again.

"What was that?" I ask, in utter shock at what was now the greatest memory I possessed. Not in my eighteen years alive or my twenty dead had I ever thought that was scientifically or mystically possible.

"I'm sorry, I couldn't hold myself back any longer..." he says, breathless. I wonder what he felt in the midst of our embrace. Was he rendered winded from the intensity of the kiss, or could he actually feel me, alive in those few seconds, offering me his breath.

"No, I don't want you to hold yourself back. I have to ask though, what did you feel? What did I feel like?" I stutter through my questions, my curiosity getting the better of me.

He looks me up and down quickly, as though he's trying to decipher where my head is. I wish him luck because my mind is moving through thoughts so fast I can't even follow them. "Well, at first it didn't feel like anything. But after a few seconds it was like you were appearing under me, like slowly you became tangible... real."

I don't look away from him, I'm too engrossed in every hesitant word.

"You became real, not like the other times we touched. Then it was like I was touching thick, electric winds. I could feel your heartbeat... or maybe it was mine... but in any case you were warm and soft. Almost like you were alive again," he chokes through this last sentence. I want to reach out and hold him, anything to bring back the sensation, the excitement. I know he doesn't fully understand but his words cause a shift in my thoughts, a realization that from the moment we touched hands, he was leading me back to life while I continuously fought for my revenge.

It is so blatantly obvious that I want to scream at myself for being so blind. I realize now that I was too wrapped up in killing that man who murdered me and finally finding peace with my vendetta settled - if that's even possible. Everything changed after meeting Kian, he saw me as more than just dead. He saw me as a "person" capable of much more than my all-consuming revenge plot. As I think back to our first day, to ice skating, and our simple conversations walking the streets, I realized I never in those moments though about my murder. He transported me by the touch of his hope back into the world of the living. He always seemed to bring me back to earth, regardless of how far I strayed or how much I tried to deny him.

"I love you," I state, unable to stop the words and yet completely unafraid of them. They were true and I would not hide from them any longer.

For a moment I simply see panic, but instead of worrying myself I wait for the words to sink in. Soon acceptance, or something like it creeps onto his face, relaxing his features to the idea. There is a decided look in his eyes which releases some of the tension in the air around me. For now, he doesn't have to say it back, considering how sudden it was. I'm satisfied as it is with the unspoken understanding that he feels the same way. Five minutes ago we were a mixture of tension and uncertain anger just being around each other. I take a deep breath and turn my attention back to the movie, which is really just white noise and empty imagery to the materiality of what just took place. There's a whisper of completeness in the air now as we sit through the rest of the movie. Like everything is finally blossoming into a natural course where we just fit together, disregarding me being dead and him, not.

But I don't let myself dwell over this now. The time will come when we have to deal with this major... situation... but not now. I just want to relish in this moment and the new, welcome feeling of being centered. Of being held down by his gravity and made to feel myself again. I'm finally getting her back. The girl I used to be.

CHAPTER

7

It's another day, ordinary by all means, except... he kissed me yesterday and we decided before I left him at his house, after the movie, that we would talk about what it would mean for us today. I drift through the blankets of snow, practically floating in my peace. But, as the clock ticks closer to striking the time we will meet, the gravity of the situation finally hits me. I catch sight of Kian waltzing down the street in his blacked-out jeans and a hoodie. His starkly beautiful contrast to the purity of the snow sets a fire inside me. I work to put it out, needing to stay focused and semi-objective.

He smiles when he sees me but it fades into concern, as it often does with me. Clearly I wear my anxiety as plainly as the white gown I've sported for twenty years. "What's the matter?"

I'm startled by the question but answer honestly despite that. "I'm just worried about what this could mean for us... if it's what you truly want..." I murmur, my voice as crisp as the wind ruffling his styled hair. With eyes drawn to the gentle dance it does, I feel a pang of spite that I can't run my hands through it. The grief of death means so much more now that I've found him, and something deep inside me wishes to hurry up and reverse what that evil man did all those years ago. It's not fair what he took from me, but as I gaze into Kian's crystal blue eyes, a ghastly fact stuns me into a trance.

Had I not been murdered, then, most likely, Kian and I never would have met and, even if we did I would be far too old for him. However, with reality being what it is, we have met and though I may be a thirty-nine-year-old ghost, time stopped for me at eighteen. It is definitely an excuse I settle on, that I was trapped in both age and maturity in the moment of my death, but I reason if Kian doesn't see a problem when I bring it up, then there isn't one.

"You do understand that I would be thirty-nine had I not been murdered, yes?" I ask.

His slow response sends chills down my spine. "Yes. But, it's a different situation. You have spent thirty-nine years on this planet, but I relate to you as the same age as me, at least physically. Besides I couldn't even attempt to comprehend what death does to evolutionary maturity for a ghost rather than a living adult."

I nod, my gaze darting away from him. I don't know what to say. Some of me still thinks this is all too good to be true and that he's going to run away again, just like I did. "Even if the age difference doesn't bother you, I'm still dead."

He sighs. "Maeve, stop trying to convince me you aren't worth it. Yes, you are unimaginable, unruly, and in no way could I have foreseen having you in my life, but you are apart of my life now. I am so sorry I made you question my feelings for you, but I want you to know that they have been there from the moment I met you on that road-"

"So it doesn't bother you that I am dead! If we chose to spend the rest of our lives together, you don't mind the fact that you would grow old while I stay trapped in this grayed, supernatural youth that will be irregular and uncertain?"

"Of course it bothers me, but I'm sure there's something we can do, together we can surpass anything…" he mumbles this last part as though he's not entirely sure, but wants to be. I don't blame him for his hesitancy about the inexplicable options ahead of us.

Suddenly, I'm drawn into a trance as a voice from my past sings in my head and as it does, I speak the words, unknowingly. "It is possible to bring the dead back to life, just not in the way everyone assumes." My voice sounds strangely prophetic with a hint of *her* voice.

"What?" Kian asks, dumbfounded. His tone snaps me back and I hurry to explain.

"Well, uh… a little while after I died I met this witch in New Orleans who was teaching me ways to revive myself, but we went separate ways before she could finish telling me what I needed to do," I nearly whisper, the memory of the old woman's face sets a depressing weight in my chest and causes the energy around me to dim. Kian watches my conflict helplessly, lifting his hand to comfort me. He quickly lets it fall back to his side, knowing it will only cause me more pain, unable to feel the warmth of its consolation. Shaking my head as though that will help get rid of my depression, I look back at him and smile helplessly. "I don't know how it's possible. I don't know what it would cost or if we would even want to do it, but I thought it better to suggest it than to not…" I stumble, hoping he sees how hard I'm trying and how much I want to live again, to be with him.

"Should we at least try?" Some hope emerges from his sadness. "I mean, how does one find someone capable of something like that? It's already crazy that witches really do exist, as you said, but where would we even go about finding one? And in Ann Arbor at that?" Shrugging his shoulders despite my lack of response, a new found vigor lights his eyes. "The internet will probably have something we can work off of."

"You want to try? What if it doesn't work?" I petition, my voice meek and barely audible.

"If it gives us a chance, then I would do anything," he replies, his cheeks turning a flattering shade of red.

My lips part into a smile and I nod. "Let me tell you more about the witch I met–" and off I go, telling him about the crazy woman with her theories and stories of the supernatural, only slowing when I reach the part about the boy she helped come back and how she summarized the process.

"That really isn't much to go on…" Kian says, tapping his index finger to his chin in an enticing display of concentration. "Why don't we go back to my house, I have a computer that we can use to research this witch of yours and maybe find one of our own."

I don't say anything but he knows I agree as I follow his quick steps across the street, heading towards his home. The chilled air sends anticipatory energy that sparks about me. I can tell Kian feels it too as goosebumps grace his otherwise flawless skin. With inspired dedication, it doesn't take long for us to escape into his bedroom and hurriedly pull out his laptop. A browser window pops onto the screen sending a blueish hew onto Kian's face and I watch in fascination as he navigates this technology.

Wide eyed I watch him type the words WITCHES NEARBY. There is a spinny thing on the corner and suddenly a whole new page pops up with search results counting in the hundreds. I can feel his gaze on me now but it takes me a moment to pull my eyes away from the discovery to glance over at him.

"What?" I ask him, a nervous giggle in my throat.

He grins and a blush graces his cheeks once more, something I find extremely attractive. It reminds me how inconvenient it is to be dead. "Nothing, you're just cute when you are seeing something new. Your eyes get wide and your lips... sort of droop open..." he draws off, his eyes flitting to my lips as he speaks.

Feeling brave enough to test our limits, I lean in until I can feel the heat of his wanting energy. For a moment we allow ourselves to stay in this blissful kiss, but too soon we pull apart.

"I will never get tired of that..." he says in a whisper.

"I won't either, at least until it's the real thing," I reply.

He looks at me with glorified joy drawn across his face. "Is it really possible?" he almost implores.

"What other choice do we have than to believe it is?" I gesture with a shrug. He bites his lip and I have to contain myself so I look away. I don't want to get his hopes up too high about this. A substantial amount is unknown and it weighs on me that this could go completely haywire. "So what did you find?" I redirect our focus back to our active search. If I think too much about it, I'll talk myself out of it.

"Umm, there doesn't seem to be much, especially nothing that is actually helpful. But there is this one woman who caught my interest," he says as he tracks his finger over the pad of the computer and clicks on the desired "link". The headline reads **ANN ARBOR WITCH CURES CANCER THEN VANISHES!** After a moment he starts to detail the information on the page. "Her name is Meredith and it looks like she practices natural magicks. The article says she helped cure someone of cancer a long time ago. That's what got her recognition. People's belief started to fade when neither she nor the patient would come forward. When people in the surrounding area discovered the patient was Meredith's granddaughter they continually encroached on their lives and apparently the reporters wouldn't leave them alone. Meredith freaked out and her and her granddaughter, Saoirse, went into hiding," he says, reading over the article again.

"I think I'd be angry too if people barged into my private life like that..." I say, a twinge of sympathy in my tone.

He nods in agreement then turns back to the article, pointing at it. "And look! They posted what seems to be an address!" The antagonising screen seems to glow brighter and accentuate the numbers and letters filling out the page.

"Perfect, we should go tomorrow, since it's getting late," I comment, gesturing to the window.

"Yeah, that sounds good." Kian closes his laptop and scoots on his bed until his back is pressed against the frame. We simply stare at each other for a while until we are shocked out of silence by the slamming of his front door.

"Who's home right now?" I ask him, immediately nervous. I wish I could kick myself for being stupid, it's not like whoever it is will be able to see me.

He chuckles a bit but I can tell he was shocked by the sudden intrusion too. "Probably just my dad," he says, lifting himself off of the bed and opening the door to his room. "Dad? That you?!" he yells into the dark hallway.

"Yeah! Didn't mean to scare ya! Just got back from some errands!" the invisible gruff voice responds.

I feel a shiver down my spine and the air in the room chills when a hint of recognition pierces my being. Needing to know, I throw myself across the room, a sudden wind picking up and thrusting me out of the instantly suffocating room and into the darkened house, towards the light at the end of the stairs. *Please... don't be who I think you are... please!* I beg. I don't know who I'm begging, the universe maybe, but it doesn't matter now, all that matters is making sure the voice of Kian's father doesn't belong to who I think it does.

"Maeve!" Kian yells after me, but I ignore him. My one-track mind locked on its target.

"What do you want for dinner tonight, Bud?" says the voice just as I turn the corner into the kitchen and watch the man set his paper bags filled with food onto the counter. I am frozen in place, numb as I stare at him with eyes wider than humanly possible and my stunned hatred courses through the air in violent pulses.

I can feel Kian's presence behind me and I know he's looking between me and his father, confused. But I don't care. I can't care. I have to shut it off. It's too horrible to make sense right now. I turn away from them, not even capable of looking at either right now. As I bolt from the house, walking straight through the walls of their house onto the street I fall to my knees. I'm not exactly sure how it happens, it's not like I tripped over anything, except maybe my own heartstrings as they are torn from my being. I barely hear the door slam behind me. As Kian falls down beside me, I am brought brought back to some form of coherence.

"Maeve, what's the matter?" the concern in his voice not registering any emotion in me.

"How did you not know? Why did this happen? How could he be your father?" I start spewing words like vomit across the grass in front of me.

"What do you mean? I don't understand!" he returns.

My head shoots up and I stare him straight in the eyes. The fear, sadness, heartbreak, concern all of it meshing in his eyes like a complex painting that I don't have the energy to sort out. "That man in there killed me twenty years ago. Your father murdered me," I repeat.

With these words Kian falls back into the grass, unable to look away from me. "You're lying. That can't be true. My dad's never hurt so much as a fly..." he says, the denial shooting straight through me like an arrow.

"Deny it all you want. I have to go," I say. Disgust overtakes me. How could I have fallen in love with the boy whose father killed me? Was this some trick of fate? Questions roll through my brain as I storm away from him, moving as fast as supernaturally possible until I don't even know where I am anymore. I wish I could tear myself open and destroy all the human parts of me, the parts that Kian had given back to me. I wish I could shut the human world out and give up. Give up and return to the simple task of revenge. I've been fighting for so long only for fate to play such a cruel trick on me.

The intensity of this upheaval sucks me into a vortex, almost granting my wish for escape. It feels like I am drowning in this human universe until I am pulled ashore, dropped into the black void, a place that feels more like home than anywhere else at the moment. It takes me a moment to stabilize again, my ghostly form torn to shreds by the immense energy it took for me to get here. I feel relief, similar to that felt when one is able to suck air into their lungs naturally and the weight that had formed disperses. When I'm put back together again, I notice something strange about myself. Before I was surrounded in this darkness, I was consumed by thoughts of Kian and his father, drowning in impenetrable human emotion, but here, I feel nothing. Not a single note of sadness nor shimmer of hope, I am just, here.

Aimlessly I feel myself drift through the emptiness, satisfied with the relief that comes with not feeling, not being. I float like a leaf on gentle autumn winds, content in this personal void. Is this what being at peace feels like? I wonder, my thoughts nearly forming visible letters to take up the space around me. As I drift, I notice myself drawing closer to a familiar light. I can't help but smile as it comes into view, tranquility feeling eminent. It's the first time I've been sent here without the unintentional assistance of Kian. As a result, I expect it will be my last time here. Still void of certainty, I draw near the light - just stopping inches away from the intangible passage. It feels as if it is the last thing I will ever see. But I don't care. *It's time.* Assuredly, I take a final look back and then step decisively into the light.

CHAPTER

8

hat... what happened? I call out to the void, not recalling anything that happened up to this point. I investigate the sphere that seems to keep me suspended like a hamster in a gigantic wheel. The inner surface feels like glass beneath my bare feet, cool and dangerous depending on how I take my next couple steps. *Wait! I can feel it!* I all but scream, though the words don't actually leave my lips. I step towards the ball, hoping to feel its smoothness with my hands once more, but the moment my foot lightly steps forward, the ball moves forward too. Off balance now, I tumble to the floor and hear a slight, deafening crack beneath me.

I feel my face tighten into a grimace, both because of being unusually sore from the landing and scared to assist the spidering fractures. Thankfully the break stops and I am able to return to my feet. I ensure my balance so as to not fall again. Suddenly, a sound beneath my feet, different from the creaking of the abused glass, catches my attention. I draw my eyes to the reverberating shuffles, silently gasping as I watch Kian run underneath the sphere, his image distorted by it.

Kian! I shout, though I know it's a useless venture.

"Maeve! Maeve come back please! Let's talk about this! I didn't know! I couldn't possibly have known! I know I can't do anything about what has happened, but I swear I won't let anything bad happen to you again!" I hear him shouting, his voice sounding too clear in my glass prison. His heartbreak, fear, betrayal, all apparent in his strides which falter occasionally and in his voice, thickened by tears he is not willing to shed. As he gets further from me, the ball, as if pulled by a fast-acting elastic, shoots forward, following him.

I can't do anything but try to keep my balance as it moves on its own. Never once, even when I fall for a second time, taking my eyes off of the perfect boy.

I don't know how long he runs, or how long I follow, but soon enough our pace has slowed and with a heavy heart, Kian falls to his knees, his pant legs dirty in the sodden grass. With regret I call out, *Kian! I'm not ready to rest yet! I want another chance, I want the chance Kian was trying to give me!* I yell. The words only echo silently in my sphere, never reaching an auditory level. Suddenly, his head shoots up and I see the fire in his eyes, I know what he's about to do.

Again I am flung forward when Kian bounds off into the night. He knows where to go, I can see it in his assertive pace just as easily as I can sense it in my soul. I can't help but cheer as he approaches the house, spinning with joy in the sphere. I suck in a deep breath when he slams his fists to the old door, only stopping when its inhabitants open it and reveal themselves to him.

"What do you want this late at night?" Meredith asks. She looks older now than her picture in the article, her flame-red hair dulled with dispersed grey and her face admirably wrinkled.

However, her eyes are as clear and vibrant as someone's who holds a world-full of wisdom. I watch their interaction take place. Her telling him to leave, him begging her to let him explain until finally she stepped aside and Kian negotiates himself into the house. I thought now that they were inside I would be shut out and unable to hear the rest, but to counter my assumptions, I am shot through the sturdy walls, throwing my hands in front of my face to shield from the debri that must have been made. Again, I am wrong. Together, the sphere and I mold into the dimly lit living room and remain floating near where Kian sits on a dusty, tattered sofa.

It feels like the sphere is too big for this room, but neither inhabitants seem to notice, and frankly I don't care to dwell either as I focus on their conversation. Their voices are just as clear together as Kian's was alone, making it easy to feel like I am just sitting there talking with them.

"I don't know what you want from me. I can't help you," Meredith says, her voice strained and tired.

"I understand your hesitancy but I really need your help," Kian addresses her rejection. "My... well the girl I love is dead and... I want to bring her back-"

Hearing him say he loves me makes my knees go weak and I hurry to sit on the floor of the sphere. I can't help the following flinch when the crack deepens but in hopes to remain focused on their conversation, I try to ignore it.

"Like I said..."

"Kian," he finishes for her.

"Kian, I'm sorry but I can't help you. I don't know who you think I am, but there's nothing I can do for you."

Shaking his head he presses on, not taking no for an answer. "Look, I'm sorry to be a burden, but I can't lose her. I know who you are and I know you are the only one, maybe in the whole country who can help me. Please, I'm begging you!"

I rip my eyes away from the desperate boy and my gaze hardens on Meredith. *You have to help us, help me. It wasn't fair what happened to me and now that Kian knows it was his father, he feels more responsible than ever!* I plead, trying to reason with her, despite knowing that she cannot hear me.

"Why do you think you have the right to interfere with this sort of thing? Nature and Fate are not meant to be toyed with in that way, even if it was possible," Meredith scolds him.

"We just discovered that it was my father who killed her twenty years ago, and it's my place to make it right. But even before that, I love her. I want to be with her," he says, no longer maintaining eye contact.

Meredith's posture has turned more sympathetic as she comes to understand his motives, but when she responds, it doesn't seem like she is going to budge. "I truly am sorry. It is a horrible thing and I do think you two are cosmically tied by the actions of the past. But I can't... no, I won't help you. It's not my place to get involved in fate's plan-"

"Oh what nonsense you're spouting, Grandmother," a clear, feminine voice says. I turn to face it and find a girl, maybe seventeen or eighteen coming into the room. She uses the wall for support, indicating how unwell she is, but her expression and tone don't hold a single ounce of the sickness she must carry. Her long auburn hair drapes over her thin shoulders and lovely feminine figure, her eyes a piercing grey as the bounce between Meredith and Kian.

Meredith presses her lips into a hard line. "Go back to your room and rest," she states in a commanding voice.

"What is it you have come here for?" the girl asks Kian, completely disregarding her grandmother as though she wasn't even in the room. I notice the way her expression changes when she gets a good look at Kian and I grit my teeth.

Kian hurries to stand and helps her to the seat next to him on the couch. She nods gratefully at him before he sits beside her. "I was just asking your grandmother to help me revive my dead girlfriend. It's my family's fault she's like that and I have to help. I love her," he confesses.

The girl nods. "Grandmother, we are going to help him."

Meredith shakes her head vigorously, chanting the word 'no' as though it would change her granddaughter's mind. "We are not going to do anything."

For a moment there is silence and the longer they stare at each other the stronger the tension in the room grows. I realize as I watch them that they are having a conversation, just not one we can hear.

"Then it's decided, we are going to help you."

"Thank you! Thank you so much!" says Kian, unable to conceal his surprise. Meredith's sour expression cannot dim his mood. I can tell his mind is racing with how and when questions but when he speaks again, he speaks directly to the girl.

"So, what do we need to do?"

The girl glances at her grandmother. "Saoirse no," Meredith states, her voice cold as death.

"Why don't we talk about that when we have your girlfriend here. Don't want to scare you off just yet," Saoirse says, unaffected by her grandmother.

Kian nods hesitantly, most liking considering how he's going to get me here when he has no clue where I am.

"You should leave now," Meredith commands.

The force of her words, though they were not directed at me, cause the sphere to fall into a shaking passion, cracks working their way through the metaphysical glass. In an instant, the sphere shatters completely and I fall through. With a scream, I squeeze my eyes shut and wait for the pain that comes with landing ungracefully on a solid floor. After a short stent and I feel nothing, I open my eyes only to find myself back in the black void, deprived of the sensations I had in the sphere.

"What was that?" I yell into the darkness, finally finding my voice. I don't know how long it's been since I last used it, but apparently it's been long enough that it is unfamiliar to me. My rage emanates from me and pushes the parameter of the barrier. In a flash the blinding white light appears in front of me.

"You must rest now," the familiar cacophony of voices hums, whipping me like a ferocious wind as it cascades the light about me once again.

"I'm not ready, I want another chance!" I bellow. I'm sure if I had vocal chords they would be tearing with the force of my passion.

"You wish to stay with the boy descended from the man who took your life? We offer you eternal peace," they declare.

I'm stunned into reflection. I can't fight their pronouncement and I allow it to sink in. In all honesty, they are right. That man slaughtered me and for twenty years all I wanted was revenge. A revenge that obliterated all humanity from my "almost" existence. I roamed the earth without a shred of belief in eternal peace or confidence that I would ever get a second chance at life. But, when I met Kian, he showed me it could be different. He found a glimmer of benevolence and compassion in me, some of my human remnants. It didn't matter that I did not occupy a breathing, tangible body. He taught me, as cheesy as it may sound, to reconnect in a way that formed this bond we have shared since day one. I am not sure what to call it, whether it be love or some cosmic fate. But in any case, it made me believe I was worth a second chance.

"It seems you have made your decision," the chorus says, their tones undecipherable.

"Yes," I reply with a firm nod.

"There is no going back now, once you return you will never get this chance again. You will be tied to Earth for the rest of time, even when there is no such thing. Do you understand this?"

"I do." My proclamation is devout. I feel a suction grab at my being and magnetically pull me to the ground. It's overwhelming and I'm utterly terrified now. As I stare up at the harsh sun, unaffected by the glare of its rays with no inclination to blink, I am certain I've made the right choice. Sitting up, I look around in order to gage my surroundings and determine my next course of action. I have no idea where I am. Realizing the light offered no ease of transition I rebel with a metaphorical sigh. Standing, I begin a speedy hunt for clues. I know now that all I have is time, but Kian doesn't. I want to spend the rest of his life together before I have to wander alone for eternity.

Walking along the cobblestone streets and rounded buildings, painted in all colors, I start to have an awful sense of deja vu. When the wind blows jazz music through me I realize I've been here before, many years ago now. I round the corner and nearly run into the hordes of walking, talking, and dancing. The perfume of their lives brighten the world around them while I'm left feeling chocked up the longer I walk the streets and the closer I get to the place I hand wandered nearly fifteen years prior. Part of me wonders if I might find her there, just as mysterious and whimsical as she was the first time I saw her.

She must be long passed by now, the witch I met the last time I was in New Orleans, but the hope remains. I feel nostalgic as I move through the crowds, unable to stop myself from dancing to the music that hangs in the air. Something about this place makes me feel alive, maybe it's the supernatural history that has integrated here, the charm, the voodoo, and the magic. It feels like home here. If I could cry, I'm sure tears of my exultation would welcomingly stream down my cheeks.

"I would love to share this with Kian," I say aloud, my voice rippled with dreams. *Kian! I need to get back!* The revelation shocks me out of my hazy state, New Orleans is like a drug to me, no wonder I stayed so long back then. The rush of time comes back to me, hitting full force and I start to run. I don't exactly know where to run, so I let fate play its part. I invite it in. It has always taken me where I needed to go. My anxiety suffocates the air and I can see the people who come into contact with me, momentarily suffer the same discomfort. *Hurry please!* I beg the wind, the earth, the universe. And they listen.

CHAPTER

9

A sudden howling of wind scoops me up just as the
earth shudders and quakes violently, shooting me
into the air at high speeds. I'm off balance but it
doesn't seem to effect the wind as it blows me away from
the painted streets and drug-hazed lights. I don't know
if I am going in the right direction, but I don't fight the
wind. If anything the universe knows and is driving me
towards where I need to go. My ghostly hair, reflecting
the light of the grinning sun, snaps in the invisible wind.
As I shoot through the air, bumbling and tumbling, I start
to laugh. It's a hysterical sound created by the threat of
eternal solitude and the chance to live again. It seems I am
now above all things human and supernatural, a unique
predicament.

I'm going crazy, I think to myself as my high starts to fade and the modern world rushes into view. I'm going too fast by all measures, though I'm not really scared anymore, I just keep on letting the wind lead. The closer I come to the ground the more of Michigan I recognize. It really is a surreal place, with its greens and blues, it's nothing like the otherworldliness of New Orleans, but it has its own regal beauty that draws me to it. It's sunset by the time I reach the grassy carpet of the park and the moment my translucent feet touch the earth I start running.

I call Kian's name, maniacal with my need to find him and take him back to Meredith, of course I am less eager about the granddaughter. After what feels like an hour of screaming for him, I hear him call out my name. His frenzy matches mine when he sees me and without thinking I run into his outstretched arms. I am reminded once again of my unfortunate personage as I practically pass through him. Though it's not as fluid as it usually is when people walk through me, it takes a moment and I can feel a jab of sharp electricity, a jolt of which I know he felt too.

"I'm sorry, I should have been more careful," I scold myself and plead with Kian, his confused and pained expression telling me everything.

"No I'm sorry. I didn't know about my father's past and I-"

"And you what?" I interrupt him, wanting to relinquish his guilt. "You couldn't have known and you couldn't have stopped it."

"I know! I know... I just, I never would've brought you there, or maybe... I don't know. I never wanted to hurt you..."

I place my hand over my heart, the emotions swelling in me almost too much for this shell of a body to maintain. "Kian," after I say his name I wait until he looks up at me. "I love you and if you love me too, let's do what we can to bring me back."

"Right! I talked to that witch, she agreed to help us... well her granddaughter, Saoirse, did–"

"I know. But we have something else to do first," I say, a plan formulating in front of me quicker than I can follow.

"Okay... wait, how do you know?" his confusion forces me to laugh.

"It's a long story that involves glass spheres and "the light" and eternal peace, something we can talk about after this is all over," I laugh. Growing the courage to rest my hand on his cheek, I allow the electricity to buzz through my fingertips for a moment. "Let's go."

He doesn't say anything just looks at me with those crystalline blue eyes and walks beside me as I lead him back to his house. "You are confronting my dad, aren't you?" he asks quietly as we approach the seemingly ominous front door.

I nod. "Yes and I need your help..." considering the thing I fear and hate the most is just passed this wooden barrier. Silently, I try to maintain a certain level of compassion for him, my murderer, he is Kian's dad after all.

"Of course, I can't protect him from the things he did."

At a final agreement, he opens the front door and together we walk into the house. I wish I could hold his hand, but it has to be enough just to feel his presence beside me, for now at least.

"Dad?" he calls into the house, the air doesn't feel like it should in a murderer's house, brooding and depressing. Holding a weight that only the two involved in the crime would fully be able to discern but could be felt by anyone who entered. But then again, who really is to say what one feels like. Instead this place feels like a home, barely at that, but still a home. One with sadness and it surprises me to feel a bit of regret floating in the air. Whether that has something to do with me or Kian's long lost mother, I am not to say.

"In the kitchen!" the man of my nightmares calls back, his voice a haunting melody that sounds too much like Kian's. I force myself to be ready. There's no going back as we breach the kitchen and come face to face with him. "Hey, just finished dinner. Where were you all day?"

Dithering, he clears his throat. "Um, I actually have to talk to you about something, and I need you to be completely honest with me…" He halts. I watch his nerves and hope that his father really didn't do this grow in unison veiling his thoughts.

"It's okay. Go sit at the table," I direct him, hoping I am strong enough to guide us both through the storm that's approaching. When Kian sits, so does his father. "Ask him about when he first moved to Michigan," I say, trying to start the conversation with enough of a leading question to get the right answers.

"I was thinking... well you never really told me much about moving to Michigan." He stutters over the words.

"Oh, um... that was a long time ago. Probably twenty or thirty years," he says with a shrug.

"Come on, there has to be more than that," Kian pushes and I watch the flicker in his dad's eyes.

"Well... I was only twenty-one and it was my first time living by myself after moving out of my parent's house in California. I met your mother a year later, she was working at a print shop that actually closed down pretty soon after... anyways, she was God's gift to me after the hardships of that first year, let me tell you," he reminisces and I get the sense that we are getting closer.

"Ask him about why the first year was so tough," I emplor, my voice gothic and dreary, almost scary.

Kian glances over at me before focusing on his dad again. "Why was it a rough year? What happened?"

His dad shrugs but the expression on his face gives away everything. He seems shocked, a little anxious. "Oh, you don't want me to bore you with the details. N-normal 'first year alone stuff'" he says, air-quoting.

"Oh really? Because it seems like there's a bit more than that," Kian snaps. I can tell he is getting just as provoked as I am and I am unable to see through my own rage enough to continue supporting him through this interrogation.

"N-not really. Why did you hear something?" his father questions.

Turning it on us now is he. "Liar!" I scream, my voice taking on a power of its own, causing objects in the room to shake and fall to the wooden ground, the shattering sound all too familiar. Both men jump at the sudden assault on the room's decor but Kian hurries passed it, determined to get answers.

"Does the name Maeve Cowen mean anything to you?" Kian asks.

"Maeve Cowen?" He's still staring at the broken glass on the floor and my lips curl up in a loathing snarl. Hearing my name spoken from his lips sickens me more than our initial rendezvous. He gets up from the table to pick up the shards, in any other moment I would have laughed at the symbolic gesture. He stops when Kian stands, his chair thrown down by the speedy action, and slams his fists on the table.

"Yeah. Maeve, the girl you hit with your car then left for dead!" he shouts, wildly.

Even I can't help but flinch at his reaction, looking from him to his father. All his fear and anger has instantly disappeared from his eyes and instead I am looking into a controlled but unnatural emptiness. They seem to have lost their fire and he seems to be trapped in a time that is not the present.

"Who told you this?" Kian's father asks, not breaking eye contact for a single second.

"She did," Kian replies through gritted teeth. "She's right here. Frankly I'm surprised you can't see her, I mean it's only fair that she haunts you after what you did to her."

"That's enough, Kian."

"No it's not. Why did you leave her? You could've helped, you could've saved her!"

Regret clouds the man's eyes and I am taken aback. I never thought in my twenty years of death, seething with revenge after what this man did (or didn't do) that I would feel pity for him in this moment. "Kian... that's enough..." I whisper.

"No! Didn't you hear him! He didn't even deny it!" Kian shouts, turning towards me, but not taking his eyes off of the object of his rage.

"Son, you're talking to nothing! This is ridiculous!" Kian's dad bellows, now it's his turn to slam his fists on the table. When he does this something in the air seems to change. The room grows colder and I feel myself becoming... visible. It's unlike anything I had ever felt with Kian. this time it's my choice, my choice who sees me and who doesn't. And now, it's time for Mr. Sinclair to meet his sin.

Watching the fear creep back into the eyes of this man gives me a sick pleasure. Tilting backwards as though pushed by some strong force, he falls back into the kitchen counter, barely catching himself before taking a pitiful plummet to the floor. I don't move, I don't speak, I just allow him to take in his regrets and face the thing I know he's been lying about and hiding from the world and himself. I can see Kian watching us out of the corner of his eye. The moment his dad is able to see me becoming overwhelmingly obvious.

He is visibly wracked with guilt, terror and regret and I realize this is why I wanted this moment in the first place. There is a wave of contentment in seeing his pain and I am able to feel his remorse. He pleads with me silently for repentance and that is when it becomes clear, it's time I forgive him. I'm not going to do it for him exactly, but so I can move on. So I can take the next step like Kian had asked me to the first time we met, promising to help make me human again.

I forgive you, I mouth. Part of me is shocked that I am able to say it, another angry, but ultimately relieved. Mr. Sinclair wouldn't have been able to hear me in all actuality, but he understands my message. I see confusion peeking through the shroud of emotions swimming in his head.

"Kian let's go," I sigh, not waiting for his reply as I start making my way out of the house.

"Wait... what?" he finally gets out, baffled as he stumbles after me.

Mr. Sinclair doesn't bother coming after us as he would only be following Kian at that point. I disappeared right in front of his eyes just as quickly as I had appeared. His expression of disbelief is etched into my mind. Neither Kian or I talk, even as the distance from the house grows far enough that the air doesn't feel permeated with his energy. Though I can feel Kian's agony building as though we have been walking for miles rather than simply a couple of streets. I try to make him bear the silence until he can't hold his tongue any longer.

"What happened in there?" he questions, his rage still apparent in the underbite of his tone.

"It was time to let it go, like you said," I reply, my voice shakes and I wish I could release the tension built up in me. I wish I could cry. "We should find a place for you to sleep tonight." The mention of sleeping introduces the memory of the plans we have for tomorrow and it's as though the reminder forces Kian to acknowledge how tired he really is. *That's what I thought,* I think when I turn to inspect him and see the exhaustion painted onto his otherwise flawless features. He yawns, making me even more sure.

"Probably a good idea. But we have to talk about this tomorrow."

"Okay, after everything is over," I promise. He needs answers and I get that, I would too if I was in his position.

After a short walk, we reach what looks like a family run hotel and decide this will be the best place to stay for the night. It's short, easy work to check in and walk up the quick flight of stairs to our second story room. Once inside, Kian practically throws himself on the bed. Part of me wants to chide myself for being so careless with his human needs. When I don't move from my position at the door, Kian lifts himself upright and rests on his elbow, his head in his hand.

"You can use the bed too," he says, waving his free hand at the large empty space next to him.

I give him a half smile but carefully make my way onto the bed. It's not like I'm nervous or anything, I just can't help but see the possibilities of tomorrow and how likely it is that things won't be going our way.

As if he had read my mind, Kian lays flat on his back, turning his head to look at me. "Everything will be alright. We will bring you back." His voice sounds groggy, already half asleep.

"Go to bed," is all I can say. Within the next few minutes Kian has fallen asleep and I am left watching the way his chest rises and falls, how his muscles relax, how his face has the most peaceful expression, an expression not unlike death. I push this thought out of my mind. One of us being dead is enough. As I look at him, I scoot down the bed until my head is resting next to his. I close my eyes to allow myself to feel all the emotions I have. The world doesn't break open as my passions grow like it previously would. Instead it's as though they are accepted by the universe. I start to feel more human than I have ever felt. It feels like I've relieved myself of all the hatred and revenge I had stored over the years. Finally my eyes are open and I see what... no... who I really am.

"*I deserve to live,*" I whisper to myself. And now, I finally believe it.

10

When the sun shines through the roughly polished window, shining like a ray of hope into our eyes, Kian shuffles awake.

After a yawn and an attempt to orient himself with his location he turns to me, resting in the window nook near the warmed glass.

"Good morning," he says, his voice deep and husky.

I shiver at the sound of it but give him a smile before looking back out of the window.

"Maeve?" he questions. I hear the bed creak under his movement and then the same from the floorboards, an indication that he's walking towards me.

"I can't wait until I can feel things. I miss the touch of grass, of pencils and paper, of other people..." I murmur that last part, an image of me running my hands through Kian's hair and down his arms graces my thoughts. I smile sadly again.

"Soon... soon you can do all of that," trying to convince himself just as much as me when he says this.

"Yeah."

Why don't we head out now. You slept in and it's already pretty late, a little while after noon. So I'm sure Meredith and Saoirse are ready to receive us by now."

I nod but it takes me a moment to hop off of the sill. I just want to stare at the world in its illuminated beauty. These eyes, though dead, see a lot more than those of Kian's. Now that the drama has settled, the world sparkles and shimmers with an aura on the horizon of heaven.

"Has the world ever sparkled for you?" I ask randomly, still unable to look away from the window, even as I followed him towards the door.

He stops for a moment and waits for me to pull my eyes away to look at him and then professes. "When I met you it did. It was like a burst of lightning struck the earth and I haven't been able to see anything but sparks."

I giggle. "That's quite ostentatious."

"Maybe," he shrugs. "But it's true."

I want to kiss him. My eyes fall to his lips, a miniscule act he notices. With a grin he seems to assure me that we will be able to whenever we wish, soon.

Reinvigorated, we hurry out of the hotel and start the trek to Meredith's home, uncertain as to how all of this is going to work, but hopeful nonetheless. As we approach the door, I feel a calmness, as though there is an invisible field pushing out everything bad.

"Are you ready?" Kian asks, holding his fist up to the door, prepared to knock at my signal.

With expectancy the door opens abruptly and a familiar voice bellows. "Well she better be."

Shocked, Kian and I nearly jump away from the door as we come face to face with Meredith the Witch. "Well why are you standing there like a couple of schmucks, get inside." Before her aggression increases, we rush through the front door. Part of me is worried she'll take Kian by the collar and sock him straight in the nose for the infringement on her uncomplicated life.

"Sorry for the intrusion," I say. I am not quite sure she can hear me but she proves she can definitely see me as she blatantly stares me down with her seemingly unending gaze as I walk past her.

"It's not you who's intruding…" she mutters just loud enough for my companion to hear.

I hold out my arm to stop Kian from reacting. "Thank you for your help, Meredith, it means everything to us. To me."

I can tell she is fighting to remain respectful with me, probably an etiquette between our designations. "Don't thank me, thank my credulous granddaughter," she spouts. I can practically see the smoke coming from her ears.

"You are very welcome," says the granddaughter making a perfectly timed entrance.

I feel like gritting my teeth when I see her eyes dip to Kian before focusing on me. "So how are we going to do this?" I inquire, my immense curiosity overriding my jealousy.

"It may be best for you to sit down for this," she replies politely, glancing with a sudden nervousness at her grandmother before limping away to the living room. She seems to be sickly and struggles to settle into the plush sofa. She looks paler today, her eyes more sunken. I start to wonder how she came to be this ill as the silence drags on with the ticking of the cuckoo clock on the wall.

"That's none of your business," Meredith says from the seat next to Saoirse.

"I am so sorry! I didn't realize I said that outloud!" I hurry to apologize, looking between them both, petrified.

"Don't worry it's okay," she proclaims as she turns to her grandmother. "Yes Grandmother, it is her business if she's going to occupy this body when I'm gone," Saoirse says. She offers me a small smile then a pointed stare at the elderly woman who rolls her eyes and scoffs coldly. It's apparent that the small iota of respect Meredith had for me has faded with my obtrusive question and clearly she possess the ability to interpret my silent thoughts.

"What do you mean, *occupy your body*? " Kian asks, enunciating the last few words.

"It means exactly what *it* means." This sounds almost riddle-like, making my head spin with too many scenarios. My head would hurt by now if that was possible. With a burdensome chuckle she continues. "The only way to bring a soul back to life is to have it possess the body of a willing person. The transition into the body must be performed seconds before the host's death or both souls will be lost and the body would remain a perished corpse," Saoirse explains.

"I can't just take your body!" I exclaim, finally understanding why the grandmother loathes this idea.

The girl affirms her willingness to gift her body by shaking her head gracefully. She is stunningly beautiful even at the edge of her own approaching death. "I want to do this for you. I want to give this body a chance to live better than it was able to with me."

"But, who knows when you are actually going to… we couldn't do that to you or your grandmother!" Kian interjects. I can tell he's disgusted and wrought with guilt that he prematurely agreed to this plan.

Saoirse holds up her hand like a patient mother. The maturity she embodies likely a product of living with her illness. "There's no more discussion. The time is near and I know that tonight is the right time to complete this enchantment."

I glance over at Meredith, feeling the energy in the room grow even heavier than it had been, something I didn't think was possible. She looks aghast, though she is clearly trying to hide it. Clearly her granddaughter did not

discuss this revelation with her before we had come. With
unease I return my focus to Saorise. It's obvious that she has
made up her mind so I don't try to sway her. Out of anyone
on this planet, I am probably the strongest believer in being
able to chose our way when leaving the Earth.

"Grandmother will prepare incense and herbs to
cleanse the body in preparation for a new life." I can hear
the subtle way she almost pleads with her broken-hearted
grandmother.

"But... if you don't mind me saying so bluntly, if the
body is sick wouldn't it be pointless to put me in it only to
die again soon after?"

Meredith finally speaks up, her voice clipped. "It isn't
something explainable to those outside of the practice,
but the ceremony will revive the body entirely, healing all
blemishes and blights, no matter how fatal."

I nod though it still doesn't make total sense in my
mind. "Then why haven't you already healed Saoirse?" The
second the question is out of my mouth I regret it, but it's
too late.

Meredith tries to speak again, her face contorted with
spite, but she's interrupted by her granddaughter.

"We tried... for many years, but we were using magick
for selfish reasons, rendering it useless," Saoirse responds
before the assured string of profanities left Meredith's
mouth.

I remain silent, not wishing to further offend the only two people in this world who can help us. Besides, I know when I have said enough.

Clearing her throat, Saoirse continues. "We will start tonight, at midnight, and the ceremony will complete at three exactly, This is the time when nature's potentials are at their peak. Kian you will need to stay out of the house until Grandmother invites you back in. No matter what you hear or what mental tricks might be played on you by outside forces, you cannot come inside."

"If you do the whole ceremony will be nullified and we may all lose our lives. You are not technically considered any part of this so fate would see it as a breach of contract and punish us dually." Meredith stares directly at him, ensuring he understands his position and won't put anyone in more danger than is necessary.

"Okay, I'll comply with whatever you need me to," he says, his voice masking the apprehensive emotion displayed in his posture and in his gaze.

"Saoirse, Maeve, you two should go acquaint yourselves better. It will make the transfer easier. Not by much, but enough. Kian and I will go to the market and get the fresh herbs we need, I'm sure you don't have a problem with that?" she finishes, facing Kian.

"Of course. I'd like to see what you plan to use," he replies. I can't tell what he's thinking and that makes watching him leave with Meredith that much harder. When the girl and I are alone together, sitting in the now silent house, I take a moment to gage her. Again, she is quite beautiful even with her frailty and the clear deterioration of her body. Up close I can see a few freckles spreading a faded pattern over her nose and down her cheeks. It renders an innocence amix the maturity she portrays. Her eyes, a light grey with specks of emerald green. I am sure, at another time, they were brighter when her body was healthy enough to produce such a magnificent color. She sits straight and feminine despite the obvious pain that hardens her muscles with every slight breath or shift in position. Her nails are painted a soft nude but cannot hide the underlying greying from poor oxygen, reminiscent of a cloudy day.

"You are truly beautiful!" Saoirse says. She must have been watching me just as I was her only moments prior.

"I was just thinking the same about you," I reply. The compliment puts a distinct blush on the tip of her nose and floods faintly across her cheeks. Suddenly, a thought crosses my mind and I furrow my brows. "Why are you really doing this?"

She looks at me, contemplation written over her face before responding. "Like I said before, I want to give this body a chance to live, just as you desire for yourself."

"But that's not the whole story," I push, noting the resonance in her tone that indicates she isn't telling me everything.

She bites her lip, glancing away. "Don't tell her I said this, but... I want my grandmother to be able to keep on seeing this face, even if it isn't mine anymore. Not just as a memory, either, but alive. I want the burdens of my life to disappear when you take over." She's whispering now, unable to hold back the tears that betray her composure, sliding down her cheeks like glistening truths.

I feel my emotions swell for her, and without Kian here to keep their effect in check, a wind starts up, blowing pages of books erratically and almost knocking a vase of purple lilies off of the table. I try to calm myself. "I'm sorry, I don't know why I'm reacting like this..." I mutter, my efforts to reel in the chaos failing.

"Let it out," she replies, tears still swelling in her eyes. "It's the way you express your emotions in this state. You shouldn't feel the need to suppress them, especially not around me." her voice is kind and it causes my heart to break.

"Stop being so nice to me. I'm practically stealing your life from you!" I shout, angry with myself.

"No, you are helping me rest in peace," she argues, her face strict. "I trust you to care for this body better than I ever could. I know you will give it the life it deserves."

"But it's *yours*. I've been fighting for years to get my own back and here you are just *handing* me yours!" My intensity causes the vase to fall to the floor, the familiar shattering of glass knocking me out of my exasperation. I lean back into the seat as far as I can without falling through it, hoping to shield myself from Saoirse's steady gaze.

"You've fought for your second chance and now I'm fighting for mine. Simply put, we want different versions of the same thing." Her explanation makes sense to me; like a puzzle coming to sudden completion.

"I'm sorry," I say, dropping my head like a child who's just been scolded. "I've been all over the place today. I'm so worried this won't work and I'll have to spend the rest of my existence as an apparition roaming the earth for all eternity."

"Who told you that?" she questions, her face drawn with compassion.

"The universe, the void, the cacophony of voices, or god. Whatever it is… they were." My response seems to surprise her but she quickly brushes it off.

"Then that's more reason to make sure this is seen through from the moment my soul finds eternal peace to the moment your body is filled with the spirit of life," she states, her conviction contagious.

For the next couple of hours, we talk. She fills me in about her life, growing up sick. How every second was about survival, resilience, pain, loss, and her strength to cope with unexpected days of feeling better or worse. Then I shared my life and death with her. I was able to discuss my parents. I felt more and more human as the moments passed and it felt good. Sitting with Saoirse and talking without barriers was freeing and long overdue, as it seemed for the both of us. We cherished every word, every laugh, every cry, every broken dream, every story until there was nothing more to share. We knew each other inside and out. By the time Kian and Meredith walked back through the door, paper bags full of strongly-scented items, Saoirse and I were finally sitting in silence, a welcomed friend.

"Kian drop those upstairs and leave. It's time," Meredith says, her tone calm and collected. It's surprising to see her so apathetic this close to the moment she's been dreading. Deciding there's no point in dwelling on it anymore, Saoirse and I find ourselves standing and making our way towards the tired old lady. "Did you two get the chance to talk?" she asked.

There is a discreet hope in her eyes and I understand the last bit of hope she maintains that we have changed our minds. "Yes we did-"

"-And this is the right choice," Saoirse finishes, her voice dripping with kindness and admiration for her grandmother. "I know this isn't what you want, Grandmother, but I also know that you are sensible enough to realize it's what needs to be done."

Meredith sighs at her granddaughter and places a wrinkled, veiny hand on her bony cheek. "I know, my love." And with that she turns and starts the trek upstairs, passing Kian on his way down.

"I love you," he says as he passes me and I feel the tingle of electricity as he swipes his hand near mine.

"I love you too," I whisper.

CHAPTER

11

Those final words, that final gaze, that final blast of electricity, reminded us how soon we might be able to touch and be with each other. It drives me into the room with its windows boarded so no external forces intrude on the sacred ceremony about to take place. White candles lit and illuminate a perfect diagram surrounding the tub full of richly scented water. Steam rising from it but as I glide by, I can feel a chill from the water. It is all so surreal. Everything seems to drip with a haze like the streets of New Orleans, yet crystal clear through my supernatural eyes.

I hear a thump behind me and I force my eyes away from the intoxicating sight of the ceremonial set up to see what has fallen. I gasp as Meredith drops down to assist

Saoirse with the heavy task of standing. Everyone honors the silence that was dictated by the witch, a grandmother, before we entered this sacred space. She made it quite clear that the only things to be spoken in this chamber is the incantation for the enchantment. The gravity of the situation and Saoirse's death drawing nearer strikes to my core. In the back of my head I heard the chorus of voices warning me of what my decision would cost if we weren't successful tonight.

Not an option, I think to myself. *Failure is not an option. We are all sacrificing too much to allow it.* I hear shuffling behind me, signifying the start of the ceremony. There are no clocks in the room, but it doesn't seem like Meredith needs one to know when to start, on time.

As we were coming up the stairs to embark on this transition, I finally asked Meredith if she had ever done a successful ritual like this before. She deflected my inquiry by telling me to "go read the article". I quoted it to her then, reminding her it had said she cured someone of cancer. I tried to see how she could correlate those as the same thing. Curing cancer and bringing someone back to life. She ignored me after that, awfully silent which brought my stress levels up significantly. Without speaking Saoirse had hovered her hand over my shoulder to comfort me. Though we weren't physically touching, her hand felt solid and I reminisced over what it felt like to have the pressure of someone's hand on my shoulder.

Dressed in a fairly translucent white dress that floats about her with ghostly beauty, she glides her way into the claw footed tub. Submerging herself slowly into the herb coated water. The moment her body was covered, the room grew hot and began to smell like earth, the air sweetened. It was a mixture of the grainy soil with sweet roots and leaves lightly littering the scent of strong flowers. The water stilled with her slowing breaths. There is an expectancy in the air that makes me jump when Meredith brakes the silence with a sudden ethereal humming. She isn't singing in English but some exotic language. I come to recognize it as a blessing over Saoirse and a prayer to help her soul rest at peace. Swiftly it fades and becomes an enchantment over me. It is my soul's turn to give life to her body.

Meredith dances about the tub and me, wafting smoke through the room, concentrating it over Saoirse's body. I feel drawn to the cloud it creates and don't stop myself taking a few steps towards it. Soon I am enveloped in the haze, there alongside Saoirse.

I am silently immobilized when I see a familiar flash of light and then suddenly my vision is blurred by moving picture memories. They are so beautiful I can do nothing but stay back and watch them with a full heart. Instantly I realize they aren't my memories, they are Saoirse's. *In order for the body to start anew with no burden of a past life, one must release the memories, the scars, everything that made it what it used to be. In all aspects the body must be reborn.* The directive plays around in my head as the memories dissipate, drifting into the smoke, no longer to be remembered.

Soon after I find myself lost, stuck within the haze and trying uselessly to part the grey smog with my hands. All at once, I fly forward as though something forcefully pushes me from behind. Moments later, as I open my eyes, the world seems to sway and pulsate. I squint my eyes searching for clarity though the world remains blurry and my vision untrained. I try to move my hands to part the haze but they feel heavy, too heavy. I attempt to turn my head to see what is restraining me, but I realize it is immobile as well. Panic sets in, my lungs becoming strained, almost crushing me from within. *I can't breathe*! The terror forces out of my throat in a horrific scream that only results in liquid swiftling filling my lungs.

Am I going to drown? I wonder as my screams continue, unnatural as the pain of suffocation intensifies. I come to the conclusion that I am really drowning and wonder what this was all for.

Maeve! Shouts a muffled yet familiar voice.

What? What do you want? Can you help me? My mind races not quite certain I should trust this voice but hoping they will save me nonetheless.

"Maeve!" she shouts again, closer this time. A muddy outline of the old woman comes into view and I watch as bubbles seep from my lips and pop at the surface of the water. Seconds later there is a booming sound and I see hands reach down and grab me.

Wait… she's touching me? I feel sensations everywhere and yet I'm trapped in a motionless body while outside forces, except the restraint of gravity are manipulating my senses. I'm so confused and I can do nothing but watch as she pulls me from the water, onto the cold wooden floor.

"Breathe!" she commands and moments later there is a fiery pain on my chest. I shift my gaze downwards to see what is happening. She thumps her palms on my chest. CPR. One pump, then two, after a few more I feel like I am going to vomit. Gathering all the strength I have, I roll over and cough up suffocating water, finally drawing my first breath of fresh air. It's a lovely feeling as I gulp it into my lungs greedily. I've missed these feelings, of inhaling and exhaling, of touch, of cold and of heat. But why?

"Maeve, get up now."

I comply and pull my body, too heavy for its own good, into a sitting position. Carefully I am pulled to my feet. I feel unsteady as I try to take a step, like I haven't walked in years. My limbs shake and I can do nothing but allow myself to be assisted out of the damp, gothic room and shuffled down the hall to a sweet smelling bedroom. I sit dazed as I am changed out of my wet clothes and put into a soft dress that tingles on my skin as though tiny sparks dance across it.

"Are you comfortable?"

I stare up at the ceiling as I am laid on my back over the bed. "I'm not *uncomfortable*…" I reply, my voice is sore and the moment I speak it feels like I'm swallowing water all over again.

"Rest now…" the words, granting me permission as her hand is placed on my head and I give in to the overwhelming exhaustion. I sleep like the dead. My brain tries to start up, but something or someone seems to hold me back so I surrender and sleep longer. My muscles are sore, stiffly moving while I breathe, a sequel to my near drowning. Unconsciously, I feel my heart pulsing, pumping blood through my chilled veins. It's strange, the more I pay attention to the workings of my body the more it doesn't feel like my body. The thought is a brief one, as nearly instantaneously I feel myself finally pulled from the depths of slumber.

There is an invasive whispering penetrating the otherwise silent room. I blink my burning eyes, not used to the blaring sunlight streaming through the divide in the purple-infused curtains. The air smells like perfume with a hint of something more like cologne. I assume these scents waft from the people in the room who I cannot see, my eyes stubbornly unadjusted. Harshly, I hear a door slam and feel my ears ring at the crudeness of it.

"You're awake…" the familiar female voice says, louder now.

Slowly, I start to lift myself up, my head swimming dizzily as I do. I feel wrinkled, thin arms wrap around my back, assisting me in the difficult task of sitting up. I want to say thank you once I'm up, but that burning sensation is still in my throat, so I opt against it. I take another moment, waiting for my head to clear. The arms are still wrapped around me but I don't have the energy to care, I am grateful that they are holding me up. Much time passes before my vision clears and my muscles relax. I mobilize my strength to sit upright myself. I feel bound to my skin now, the disconnect I had felt earlier a long forgotten memory now.

"Can I get you anything?" the female voice questions, still sitting next to me. I turn to look at her.

"No... I'm alright..." my voice is still ragged but more audible now. My attention is diverted, however, when I hear the door to the bedroom open and watch a handsome young boy walk in with a glass of water and a plate of crackers. I'm nauseous just looking at the food, but conversely I am absolutely starving. I decide not to ask for it right away. The woman next to me stands and intercepts the meal. He gives it to her begrudgingly.

I watch the boy as he hands over the plate. He is obviously not aware of my penetrating gaze just yet. I feel my heart quicken the longer I stare at him and my face grows hot, a blush flushing across my cheeks. It's an invigorating sensation and I hope it looks cute and not too ruddy. Just then he turns around and his blue eyes find mine, immediately locking into place. I watch as they dilate with what I can only assume is instant longing. He ignores the woman and shoots towards me. In seconds I am wrapped up in his strong, comforting, arms.

"Maeve! I'm so glad you're awake, I've missed you. I love you. I can't believe you're back!" His words come out quick and breathless, as if touching me has set off powerful emotions in him. He presses his face into my neck and I feel the few gentle tears that glide from his eyes down my skin and tangle in the fabric of my dress. I move my hands around and grasp his back in an embrace, a comforting gesture, sensing his overwhelming emotions in this moment.

Cuddled in his arms, I feel a heartwarming reunion but I become riddled with a sense of guilt. The longer it goes on, I start to feel uncomfortable. I pat his back and release myself slowly. Never turning away from his sincerity I speak to him gently.

"I'm... I'm sorry but... do I know you?"

ABOUT THE AUTHOR

My name is KayLee Dial and I absolutely love to write because the ideas that play through my mind and the inspiration, I receive from everyone and everything around me drives my passion for bringing written entertainment to my fellow writers and readers.

I have spent the last five years really growing my strengths as an author throughout high school and even breeching into college. I was raised with a large family in Phoenix, Arizona and they have always been my biggest supporters. It is my overarching goal to reach as many people as I can with my stories, and if not be a help to them in their personal lives, maybe just be a good form of entertainment, one that they will continue turning to.

CPSIA information can be obtained
at www.ICGtesting.com
Printed in the USA
FSHW010458100921
84685FS